PRAISE FOR THE DARKSIDE WAR

"*The Darkside War* is a lean, calculated, knife-thrust of a book that provides a stellar entry-point to military science fiction."
—Nick Sharps, *SF Signal*

"[*The Darkside War* is] a lightning-fast adventure, filled with aliens, conquests, and all the technology you could ask for."
—Andrew Liptak, B&N Sci-Fi & Fantasy Blog

TITAN'S FALL

ALSO BY ZACHARY BROWN

The Darkside War

TITAN'

ZACHARY BRO

BOOK TWO OF TH

S FALL

WN

LONDON SYDNEY **NEW YORK** TORONTO NEW DELHI

E ICARUS CORPS

1230 AVENUE OF THE AMERICAS, NEW YORK, NEW YORK 10020

This book is a work of fiction. Any references to historical events, real people, or real places are used fictitiously. Other names, characters, places, and events are products of the author's imagination, and any resemblance to actual events or places or persons, living or dead, is entirely coincidental. + The text for this book is set in Bembo Infant. + Manufactured in the United States of America + First Edition + First Saga Press paperback edition March 2016 + 10 9 8 7 6 5 4 3 2 1 + Library of Congress Control Number 2015027024 + ISBN 978-1-4814-3038-8 + ISBN 978-1-4814-3040-1 (eBook)

TITAN'S FALL

1

Somewhere high over the methane seas, the jumpship hit turbulence, lurching about in the nitrogen-dense atmosphere of Titan. The churning tossed one of the eight rooks out of her seat in a flail of uncoordinated armored limbs. The alien alloys of her powered armor smacked the industrial metal floor, denting it. I looked down as she scrambled back to her seat with wide green eyes and a flurry of almost-dark hair.

Ken leaned forward against restraints. "Goddammit, we told you to *strap in*!"

We were all lined up against the wall and locked in. Everyone in armor, Ken and me babysitting all eight new additions to the platoon. Four rooks to each wall, Ken and me sitting at the front across from each other.

"Yes sir, Sergeant Awojobi!" the rook shouted, struggling with restraints.

"They gave us morons," Ken said to me, loudly enough for the whole cabin to hear. "Did you morons even go through any training? How hard is it to fucking *strap yourselves in*?"

"Yes sir," the rook mumbled, embarrassed. Everyone else

tried not to make eye contact with Ken or me. The jumpship dropped what felt like a hundred feet, my stomach shoving against my throat.

Titan was feeling punchy today.

Ken was too. "Where in the hell did you all train that we're getting such morons?"

"Icarus, sir. Dark side of the moon. Like you." The tag on her shoulder said KIMMIRUT. I was supposed to have memorized the eight names being sent to bolster the platoon, but hadn't had time to get around to it yet. Mainly because, ironically, the Rockhoppers were understrength and working overtime.

"Like me?" Ken said. "I'm *strapped in*."

I caught Ken's eye and raised an eyebrow. Dark side of the moon. Before the Darkside War, which had been more of an Encounter, Ken would not have taken kindly to the bemused "hey, take it down a notch" look I was giving right now.

But a lot had changed since then. We had an understanding.

I had to suspect Ken still hurt, deep down, over getting Sergeant First Class while I was Lieutenant of a platoon. His family had trained him to be officer class. They were fiercely loyal to the Accordance. I doubted we'd ever have been on speaking terms if not thrown into war together.

"Everyone," Ken ordered, his tone calmer, "check your restraints."

I leaned back and closed my eyes. I didn't want to lose my lunch in front of the rooks. That wasn't going to inspire much in the way of confidence. And Ken would use that against me for days. But the sour mash of standard issue Accordance protein globs in my stomach was not taking this shaking lying down.

"One hour out to Shangri-La Base," the pilot shouted

back at us from the cockpit. Alexis Hiteman had been doing bus duty for us for a couple weeks, running the platoon from point to point with gear as needed. A quiet, just-the-facts flyer, Alexis seemed to relish the chance to get to fly alien hardware by himself, without an Accordance pilot overseeing him. A new development in the Colonial Protection Forces, letting humans get their hands on more and more Accordance hardware as the fight against the Conglomerate spread throughout the outer solar system.

One of the rooks threw up. My stomach clenched sympathetically at the sound of splatter.

Alexis shouted back at us again. "It should get better once we're over the ethane lake and . . . ," he trailed off. There was a sort of "huh" sound in his voice as something caught his attention.

One of the rooks whispered a little too loudly, "It's true, the lieutenant can sleep just about anywhere. I heard he took a nap during the bombardment of Icarus crater!"

The awe was misplaced. I had been up for days straight and had nowhere to run. It had just happened. Could happen to anybody. But someone had leaked the after-action report, which included audio of me snoring while the Conglomerate ship all but destroyed the Icarus crater floor.

Ken laughed. "He's not sleeping, he's just . . ."

I opened my eyes and decided to chime in and educate them. Tell them I was about to toss my breakfast at any moment, and it was okay. Relax them a bit.

At that moment, Alexis yanked the jumpship hard right. The Accordance-made engines howled, and as we pulled massive gees, I could feel my armor compensating by squeezing my legs to force blood back up my body. It felt like a massive hand had just wrapped itself all around the lower half of my body and tried to pop me out of the suit.

"Hiteman!" I shouted.

Everyone on my side of the jumpship was hanging from the restraints, limbs sticking out straight forward, eyes bugging. Then it reversed. I was flat on my back as gravity slammed down on my chest.

The familiar thump and hiss of chaff spitting out of tubes near the back confirmed that this was not turbulence-related. Alexis was jinking hard. These were serious evasive maneuvers, the kind I hadn't felt since we first dropped into Titan.

"Alexis!" I yelled again. I kicked the armor on to pull myself forward against the force of the insanely tight turn and lean into the middle of the aisle so I could look forward through the cabin and up into the open cockpit, out into the murky amber-yellow.

"Damn!" the pilot shouted. "I got a trace, just a blip, of something out in the clouds. Came in for a closer peek so I could pass the contact info back on to HQ, thinking I could sniff a bit closer and save someone else on patrol the trouble. I'm so fucking sorry."

Sorry?

Alexis was sprinting now, the engines at an all-out howl and the entire jumpship shaking. We were moving at orbital-insertion speeds and Alexis had gone quiet again, but I could see his right hand dancing over the panels in a flurry. He was muttering into his mic.

"What the hell is this?" one of the rooks asked, his face ash-pale.

Bang! Something shook the entire jumpship.

"What we got?" Ken shouted forward.

The jumpship started wobbling violently. Alexis grunted. "Some of the little fuckers got us, one engine out."

"This is Titan, it's high ground," I said to Ken. We'd lost Saturn to the Conglomerate. Those floating jellyfish-like starships had taken the atmosphere and held it, but we had the rocks above, and Titan had been held solid for two months now. Up the gravity well, above all those other moons; this was well behind the line.

"I think we have a cricket drone swarm," Alexis shouted back. "But I'm not sure. I've never actually run into a cloud before. Just in training simulations. Never actually been in the air with them."

Point defense systems kicked on. The autoguns started chattering away.

"Can we make it to Shangri-La?" I shouted over the constant firing.

What sounded like large pieces of hail hitting the jumpship filled the cabin, and Ken and I looked at each other.

"Brace for impact," Alexis said, matter-of-factly answering my question. "I'm shutting down the other engine so they don't jam it up. It's just a matter of seconds."

Even as he said it, the roar faded into a whine and then silence. The hail-like sound continued, and then the point defense guns ran out of ammo. The whistle of Titan's thick atmosphere rushing past us was the only sound in the cabin.

"Helmets up!" I ordered as we plummeted. Mine slid up over my head and into place smoothly with the thought. The suit connected into me via some invasive alien tech, tendrils sliding up into my spine to synch nervous systems and armor.

One of the recruits started babbling on the public channel, a mix of fear and swearing.

"Get that off the public channel," Ken snapped.

"Hold your weapons tight," I said as calmly as I could. I was sure my voice quavered slightly.

We hit. My restraints snapped and I flew forward into the bulkhead. I staggered back to my feet and looked around as my brain caught up. It was dark inside and full of debris. Liquid ethane, laced with methane and propane, poured in through rents in the hull. "Mayday, HQ, anyone riding shotgun?"

"Go for HQ."

I stood up. Right before we sank into the ethane lake, I could see the tiny hump of a distant hill. Alexis had ditched us as close to solid ground as he could. "Everyone, secure your weapons and get out."

In the cockpit, Alexis lay crumpled forward, spine twisted. He hadn't been in armor. Ethane gushed in around him as the jumpship settled further and then stopped.

We were in the shallow end of the ethane lake.

"HQ, we're down. Our pilot ditched. Said it was crickets."

There was a pause on the other end. "Coordinates?"

I read them out. "How long for backup?"

"There shouldn't be anything out there, Lieutenant" was the response.

"We need evac and support nonetheless," I said.

"Twenty minutes" was the terse response.

I broke out of a gap in the hull and pushed through helmet-high water. Ken stood farther up the shore ahead of me, hip-deep in it. "Get to shore! Come on!"

He wasn't shouting or berating, Ken was calm under pressure. But he knew what needed to be done. We needed visibility, and quick.

"Alexis?" Ken asked.

"Dead. I want a headcount and weapons count," I said to Ken as I looked around. Far overhead, Titan's permanent layer of haze seemed to cap the orange thickness. And the hydrocarbon-rich clouds below that hadn't vomited out the enemy.

Yet.

"All eight accounted for. Five of them held onto their gear."

The recruits were slogging up onto the shore.

"Who're the squad leaders?"

"Tony, Yusef, raise your hands," Ken ordered over the public channel. They did so.

"Squad leaders, take point," I replied. "The three of you without weapons, fall into the center as the rest of us fan out. Yusef, your squad looks up to the clouds. Tony's squad watches the lake."

"Shouldn't we get back into the jumpship for our weapons?" someone asked.

"We stay the fuck put," Ken growled.

They were nervous. Jumpy. Scared. The Accordance had Titan swept. Orbital defenses in the form of thorny-looking platforms in orbit above us. None of this should have been happening and we all knew it.

"You mayday out to HQ?" Ken asked, private channel.

"Twenty minutes out," I replied. "They said nothing should be out here."

"Well, something is damn well out here and we have to deal with it," Ken replied.

I walked around so that each of the recruits could see me checking them over. On the public channel, I cleared my throat. "Listen up! You've heard this before but let me repeat it: There are many aliens out there. They come in all sorts of shapes and sizes. There are five aliens we need to worry about right now to survive the next twenty minutes before help comes.

"Drivers: They're cat-sized and scaly. Those pronged rear feet will sink into the flesh of your back and hook on. That pink ratlike tail? Once it plunges into your spinal cord, you're a brain-dead meat puppet at its total and utter disposal."

The placid liquid ethane on the other side of the jumpship started to boil.

"Trolls: Yes, they look like rhinoceros that stand on two feet. Either of which could stamp you into a puddle. That bio-armor? Nothing short of depleted uranium gets through it. Keep out of the way."

Insect-like forms swarmed and thrust their way through the lake, surrounding the jumpship as they schooled in our direction.

"Raptors: Our enemies decided that a velociraptor with a brain, thumbs, and a running speed of a cheetah wasn't good enough, so they made cyborgs out of them. They smell like chicken if you hit them with a laser."

Tiny wriggling metal legs glinted in the dim light as they began to surface and skip over the ethane at us.

"Crickets: These insect-like robots are the first wave. The winged variants provide air support as well. Shoot them to bits. But watch out, because the leftovers reassemble as needed. So make sure the bits are really, really tiny, and then shoot them some more. Those of you without weapons, stomp them!"

I didn't have time to talk about Ghosts. The masters of it all. Covered in advanced adaptive camouflage, running the battle in secrecy. Nor was I even allowed to tell these recruits what the Ghosts really were.

"Remember your training!" I shouted as the cloud of crickets churned out of the water to the shoreline. "You know what to do:

"Kill them all!"

2

Ken sat with his legs hanging out of the side of the hopper's open door. It had been chewed up on the approach, holes burned through the skin, but it was still flying. A trio of mantaships surrounded the hopper. Heavy air support.

"That was amazing!" Ken said over the private channel. "There's nothing left but cricket pieces back there."

I sat next to him. We'd both been the last ones in before air support started pounding the crickets.

"Twenty minutes. All we did was not die for twenty minutes."

Ken's helmet turned toward me. "We were warriors! We kicked their ass for twenty minutes."

I picked a piece of cricket out from between my boots and tossed it out over the Titan plains.

"Victory is victory," Ken said. "Enjoy the win."

We rattled in over the Shangri-La basin, scooped out of Titan's surface some thousand years before by a very, very big chunk of rock that hit hard enough to release megatons of force and leave an appropriately sized several-mile-wide crater. Then Titan's thick atmosphere had gone to work on it, smoothing and shallowing out Shangri-La into its current gentle shape, though still surrounded by blunted hills.

The Accordance buried their fortress down in the basin's hills, and now was building anti-spacecraft weapons in the protection of the basin. Each weapon was the size of a skyscraper, four needles aiming ever upward, and much of it still in the middle of construction.

I was jittery. I wanted to shuck my armor and take a long shower. I was tired of living in underground warrens and ethane lakes and amber light and Jupiter and aliens and war.

"What the hell is that?" Ken asked.

I looked over and instantly spotted what he was referring to. As we crested the Shangri-La hills and skimmed over the basin, the hopper had to curve around the vast body of a ship. It didn't look like any of the mantas or troop transports we'd been shuttled around the system on.

The heart of the ship looked like a quarter-mile-long seed with a deep black skin. A long spine further stretched out in the middle of the air forward and to the rear, a bony-looking structure with gridwork encasing it. Misty clouds surrounded that, held in by an outer transparent shell. And for hundreds of feet even more out past that hull, a second shimmering cloud hung in the air, hinting at yet another layer of ship, maybe held in place by force fields of some kind.

I clomped forward as we skimmed over the artificial clouds, and got the pilot's attention on the public channel. "What is that thing?"

"Pcholem ship," the pilot said from behind an emergency respirator. Her skin was peeling around it from exposure to whatever raw hydrocarbons had leaked inside. She should have been in a full encounter suit, but pilots this far from the action hated the bulky interference. It also may have been that she didn't have time to fully suit up, scrambling fast to get to us. "Personnel drop."

There were thousands of figures disembarking from ramps, more vehicles and equipment coming off the massive ship. All joining the tens of thousands of human contractors here on Titan, digging out bunkers for the base, drilling down into the deep rock.

A constant stream of hoppers and jumpships flew in and out, the jumpships heading for orbit, the hoppers for other distant points of Titan.

"We'll need to talk to the pilots on base about Alexis," Ken said as the hopper flared to slow down. "Tell them they need to make sure they're going out in flight suits, see if they can get crash protection gear. Let them know hostiles are slipping down. Just in case HQ doesn't think it warrants a mention."

"Yes, but we also need to ask if they'll be holding a memorial." Ken always focused on the practical. "We need to pay our respects. Alexis paid the price. And got us in close to shore, where we had a good chance."

"Right."

A whole division of the Colonial Protection Forces quartered here. Almost nine thousand armored soldiers. There were more human forces deployed around Titan, but the bulk of them were around Shangri-La.

Welcome home, I thought as we kissed dirt. The Accordance had wanted all this for themselves, no humans out past the moon, the point we'd been unable to cross by ourselves before the Accordance came to Earth.

But now that the Conglomeration had found Earth and the solar system, now that war was in full swing, human workers were everywhere toiling away for the Accordance.

It was necessity. All the planets I'd memorized as a kid, if I just reversed the names, it became a list of places the Conglomeration had taken for itself over the last three months. They'd pushed everything back to Saturn, where we held the moons and bombarded it constantly.

The Accordance needed human boots. And the Icarus Corps, built out of the Colonial Protection Forces, was still being trained and built up.

But the Accordance didn't really trust humans fully. The squid-like Arvani who held the top spot in the Accordance truly didn't regard humans with much more than disdain. We were often left guarding supply routes, protecting machinery. Like the massive weaponry being built here in Shangri-La to safeguard Titan.

Rumors were, something big was being planned for Saturn. Maybe a steady asteroid barrage or nukes. But all of Earth would just be a speck on Saturn's windy clouds. How could you attack something so vast?

Down in the bunkers, barracks lit by eerie Accordance bioluminescence embedded in the walls, I met up with the rest of the platoon. Most of them were waiting in the common room for us, lounging on utilitarian cots. News had spread quickly.

At the front, squad leaders Min Zhao and George Berkhardt jumped up. I nodded at them. "Any of you have a pad?"

Min gave me hers, and I fingerprinted in and snagged my dossier and then looked back at my new additions. They were snapping their helmets back down, and I was looking at tired, relieved faces.

Most of them were older than me. But they seemed younger somehow. And they were looking at me expectantly.

"Tony Chin?" I called out, glancing down at the pad. The squad leader raised a hand. "Over to my left."

He took a few steps over. I glanced at the pad. "Maria Lukin, Lilly Taylor, Yakov Ilyushin, over to Sergeant Chin. Rockhoppers, meet the new Charlie squad! Now, Yusef Obari?"

Yusef likewise raised a hand.

I waved to my right. Yusef moved over. "Aran Patel, Mohamed Cisse, and Suqi Kimmirut, join Mister Obari. Rockhoppers, this is Delta squad." I updated our documents.

Berkhardt moved up. "I can help you with your armor," he said to Tony. "You can call me Chef."

"Chef?"

"George Bork-Bork-Bork Berkhardt," Min Zhao explained.

Berkhardt shrugged. "I can't cook for shit, but I speak a little Swedish. And Sergeant Zhao is 'Max.' Should be obvious where we got the nickname."

"Everyone shuck down and clean your armor, stow your weapons," Ken ordered. "If you have any questions, Chef, Max, or me are here. We have bunk beds ready, look for your last name on the rack. We don't have a dedicated shuckdown room, you take your armor off and plug it in next to your bunk. You're never more than a quick sprint away from your armor, got it?"

"Yessir!" they chorused.

I had been looking over Alpha and Bravo squads. Zizi Dimka, Chandra Khan, and Lana Smalley under Sergeant Berkhardt for Alpha. Sergeant Min Zhao's Bravo squad included Greg Vorhis, Jun Chen and Erica Li. That was almost everyone.

"She's not here," Ken said, seeing me survey the platoon.

"I know."

"She's supposed to be here."

I grunted. "I know."

Erica Li was telling the new platoon members they should turn over any food they'd smuggled in to her. "I'll get them into the platoon safe. That shit is in high demand around here, and unless you've got it locked up, people will steal it. They're that sick of alien dog food."

"If you don't handle it, it will go up the chain," Ken said. "It has to."

"I'll go find her," I snapped.

One of the new platoon members gingerly pulled a chocolate bar out and handed it over to Erica.

"I'll deal with that," Ken said, jerking his head in the direction of the chocolate bar.

"Right." I turned for the stairs up to the surface.

Behind me Ken shouted at Erica. "Froyo! Hand the chocolate back over. Taylor, there is no safe down here for food. *Come on*."

I found Amira at a northeast hilltop, perched on a slab of rock, watching a hundred or so contractors in simple EVA suits working away at an EMP turret. The gun was a fifty-foot-long barrel with power cables as thick as a car running off down the nearby tunnel, which itself sank deep under Shangri-La.

The barrel had yet to be winched into place.

From her perch I could see the whole Shangri-La basin as well as the job site, now dominated by the cloudy shells of the Pcholem starship sitting the middle of it all.

"You ignoring the platoon open channel?" I asked her.

"I was busy. Welcoming the newbies is not high on the priority list. We talked about this." Her armor was streaked with dirt and peeling paint. What hydrocarbon-filled lakes had she been mucking around in?

"We hit a cricket scout cloud coming back. Lost the jumpship. Lost Alexis."

Amira stood up and turned to look at me. The name patch SINGH was missing its S.

"I told you they'd be coming here," she said.

"Could be a fluke," I said. "Accordance holds orbit. The surface was cleaned before we got moved here, before we lost Saturn. Maybe the crickets snuck through."

"No," Amira said. She stepped close enough that I could see her face behind the helmet. The silvered nano-ink tattoos were bright against her brown skin, and her eyes flashed like a cat's as light caught them. "I can taste them, they're out there, just on the edge. Accordance security says I don't know what I'm talking about, but I think our systems here have been compromised. They won't let me get in and audit them. They don't want humans sullying their systems."

"We're not trained—" I started, trying to bleed some of the anger out. She interrupted me.

"I've been playing with Accordance networks and tech for years. It's better but not infallible. You know that. The Conglomeration snuck past them to get to the moon, and that wasn't supposed to happen. And we took the hit for that."

"I know." I thought back to watching the jellyfish-like Conglomerate ship hovering over our training base. The flash of explosions. Stepping over all the corpses of recruits, reaching for emergency oxygen, the crystalized eyes.

Only three of us survived: Amira, Ken, and me. The heroes of Icarus Base. The survivors of the Darkside War. The three humans who took down an entire Conglomerate starship ourselves.

But it hadn't been just the three of us. There'd been all the others who'd died helping us.

And the new squads who'd died during the drop onto Saturn. And the retreat from Saturn.

"I was hoping you'd come say hi to the fresh meat like everyone else," I said.

"Then you should have ordered me."

"Yeah," I told her. "I should have. But you don't ever listen to me when I do that."

"Well, just because the Accordance has leverage on you through your parents back on Earth and can promote you to be Pet Lieutenant doesn't mean I have the same strings on me. But keep playing your cards right, you can be an Accordance lifer."

"Fuck you, that's uncalled for," I shouted. "The Conglomerate is the worst threat. I'm here to make sure Earth survives."

"Then do you want me sniffing out the Conglomerate threat, or dancing to orders because it makes you look good to HQ? Do you want me to pull back? We're the only platoon out here with a dedicated intelligence officer. I may be under you in rank, but we know what I am. I can go anywhere else and run intel for them, and they'd trip over themselves to have me. I expect this rules-following shit from Ken, not you."

Why the hell did this always have to be so hard? "It's not rules," I explained. "You need to know some of the names and faces who will have your back in the next firefight. They need to know you. That's how it works. We're trying to fashion a team out of all these human bits and pieces. I'll block for you while you go hunting, I just want you to take support with you, get them used to working with you. Alternate the new squads in and out daily while you prowl. I want someone to have your back, is that so wrong?"

Amira turned and looked back out of Shangri-La. "You know, I could be jumping at shadows. Don't put yourself out there on my behalf, I can take the yelling if HQ gets pissed. Say I did it against your recommendation."

"You and I both know there are a lot of shadows out in the universe that want us dead," I told her. "Take the squads with you. I'll hold the linc."

3

Armored up and fresh after a day down, I took the Delta squad out for a roll with Alpha alongside. The new additions were adjusting to Titan gravity and getting a little jumpy. Which was understandable. They'd come screaming down out of orbit in a hurry, been shot out of the sky by Conglomerate crickets, stood their ground by a propane lake, and then flown into Shangri-La, where'd they'd met an unimpressed platoon.

Now it was time to stretch their legs and keep their attention focused forward. Amira had taken the other squad out past the hills on one of her glitch hunts, though she hadn't told them that. I'd ordered her to take them with her.

Far, far under our feet as we bounded about the Shangri-La plain, the civilian contractors worked to tend the heart of Shangri-La: an Accordance-made dark matter generator, half a mile deep in the rock. This would power everything from our EMP cannons to the skyscraper anti-spacecraft weapons, which we were told could vaporize a rock the size of Manhattan dropping on us.

Which led you to wonder if there would be any on their way anytime soon.

"The Canadian from up near the Arctic, Suqi," I asked Ken, her wide eyes flashing back into memory, "she got bounced around. Is she okay?"

"Physically. She's still a bit wary of me, I think," Ken said.

"You've watched too many movies. Leadership isn't just yelling."

"And you need to stop letting them stare at you like some movie star," Ken shot back. "You need to give them some tough orders, make them realize what it is we're in the middle of. We need them to be ready, not starstruck."

A message from HQ pinged and scrolled down in the lower left of my helmet's visor. A request for a meeting. "Damn. HQ."

"Yeah?" Ken asked.

"They want an in-person."

"I can have Chef take lead and come with you," Ken offered.

"Nah." I shook my head, even though Ken couldn't see it. There was friction between me and Ken, no doubt. And we'd buried most of it back on the moon. But I still didn't want him to stand there and watch me get chewed out for something he'd warned me would be a problem with that "see, I told you so" look on his face. "It's Amira. They're going to chew on my head a bit, no reason for you to get backsplash. Plus, I need to get Shriek back to our barracks. Keep showing Delta the terrain. I want them to be able to bounce around the basin with their eyes closed. Every loose rock—"

"Every loose rock and every hidey-hole," Ken interrupted, completing the sentence.

\+ + + +

HQ, like our barracks, was just under the surface. So we could boil out on the basin like cockroaches from our crevices if the Conglomeration came at us. It was farther into the center of the basin, underneath the bulk of the Pcholem spaceship that had landed and come to dominate Shangri-La.

Major General Foster didn't spend a lot of time armored up; he was in Colonial Protection Forces gray BDUs, which almost matched the gray coming in at the temples, and he had a perpetually tired look. He stared at me as I clomped into his office. Behind him on the wall was the Icarus Corps logo, the moon and an Earthrise, surrounded by a sawblade-like sun.

Usually, shit ran downhill. Foster would yell at someone lower in rank, and then on down, and eventually a company captain would end up nervously having a "chat" with me. But most of the CPF captains had come in after I'd fought the Conglomeration at the Icarus crater. They didn't want to shout at the hero of the Darkside War.

So now I was standing in front of a major general.

"Lieutenant: why the hell are you wearing armor in my office? You can barely fit through the door."

"Rockhoppers shuck for sleep and showers," I told him. "Never more than ten feet from armor."

Foster stared at me. "You telling me you don't trust how secure my base is?"

"Rockhoppers shuck for sleep and showers," I repeated neutrally.

We stared levelly at each other. Foster may have been my superior and my elder. But my Rockhoppers didn't shuck for anything but sleep and showers.

"Fuck it. I really want to talk about Sergeant Amira Singh," he said, a sour look on his face.

HQ was a giant circle filled with pie slice–shaped offices.

What looked more like the bridge of a spaceship occupied the center: consoles for comms, massive holographic displays with maps of Titan and Shangri-La, as well as theater maps of the whole system. Soldiers coming in and out from various parts of Shangri-La. When I shuffled around Foster's office, I turned my back to all that.

One thing I liked about it: few aliens over us. Our overlords, the Accordance, had basically given Shangri-La over to human oversight.

To Foster's oversight.

Foster didn't like me. He'd worked hard to get human oversight. He'd worked hard to get the Arvani off his back and he didn't want that to change. I was something that might fubar everything he'd gotten set up.

"Amira is—" I began.

"I've explained," Captain Foster said, tapping his glass desk. "You've agreed. She can't be haring off on some intuition based on her unauthorized networking and hacking abilities. I said no unnecessary trips out past our defensive coverage."

"Absolutely, sir," I said, as flat and mechanical as I could.

For a month, Foster'd been demanding that Amira focus on beefing up security. Adding trips to the network against outside interference.

But she'd been doing her own patrols. Heading out past the basin, scouring the plains and lakes in her spare time.

"In two weeks, the farms below go operational. We become a real damn fortress here on Titan. Supplies can't be hit." Foster worried about that a lot. "With EMP cannons up, the anti-ship batteries, our emplacements on the hills, we are Fortress Shangri-La. We have ammo foundries now. Foundries. We are dug in like a tick on the ass of Titan and we will not be dislodged."

"I get that, sir."

"I don't want a loss of focus. Everyone stays behind the walls. Secure. Safe. We destroy anything that comes over the hills. We keep beefing up the hills. The aliens trying to kill us won't be able to touch us. And the aliens that took over Earth, well, maybe they'll leave us alone as well. This is important!"

That was new. I hadn't pegged Foster, a lifer, as having any ill will toward the Accordance. He was old enough to remember Occupation. The accommodations Earth had made to the aliens as they came down to Earth and changed everything.

Apparently, he saw this base as a place to carve out some space from the Accordance.

That made Foster somehow slightly more likable. I wasn't a lifer. I'd been forced into the CPF because my parents were pacifist protestors against Accordance rule. Join the CPF and they lived under comfortable house arrest. If I hadn't, they would have been executed.

"If you don't rein Sergeant Singh in," Foster warned, getting back to the subject. "I will. Demote her, toss her in a brig, something. I'm done. I have no more patience. Shut her down."

"Absolutely, sir," I said, lying through my teeth.

Up from HQ a level, several carapoids had trundled down out of the Pcholem ship. The pony-sized beetles thudded as they walked, natural armor making them something you gave a wide berth as they unloaded new batches of armor onto carts.

Old-fashioned manual labor: a carapoid could easily lift all several hundred pounds of an entire suit of armor.

Several of the carapoids had chiseled symbols on their backs. Swooping letters and what appeared to be umlauts to my human eyes. I'd never seen that on the carapoids down on Earth. They'd been painted official colors, depending on their roles in the Accordance, to match the uniforms of other Accordance members.

I hung back a bit, thinking to ask, but the carapoids kept busy and didn't slow for an instant as they trucked back up toward the surface. They'd by cycling into the outside without any gear. The carapoids could fold their carapaces tight to themselves and pass up to an hour in some extremely hostile environments. I'd seen them fighting hand to hand out in the clouds of Saturn when stripped of suits by the enemy.

I ranged through a few more tunnels, nodding and stepping aside for officers.

Shangri-La's medical facilities were located inside a spotless white cavern. The Accordance didn't see much point in private rooms for general care; most of their technology resided in the ovoid pods stretched in rows by the hundreds. The floors were grilled, the better to flush away any fluids, and could heat up to render the floor sterile again.

A couple of nearby pods were open, the articulated cutting arms inside flung open, as if the moving sculpels wanted an embrace.

I instinctively veered away.

"Do you require medical assistance?" a voice asked in Mandarin, Spanish, and then English.

I turned. A struthiform had approached me from behind. I'd never really shaken the image of them as somewhat stoic ostriches in Roman armor but with velociraptor-clawed legs that could gut you in a split second.

"I am looking for Shriek, of the One Hundred and Fourth Thunder Clutch," I said. "He's assigned to my platoon."

The struthiform cocked its head, feathers near its beak

shifting as it did so. I could hear the pitched squeak from it before the flattened box on the collar near its throat spoke, translating an alien birdlike language to English for me. "I do not know a Shriek," it said. "And that clutch no longer exists. What do you truly need, human?"

I sighed. "Shriek is the one that refuses to learn names or give them. He has prosthetic limbs, and facial reconstruction, he . . ."

"Oh. That one. Yes, we are ready for him to return to you."

The medic led me through to the quarantine wing, where there were actual offices and private rooms. A group of struthiforms clustered around a display, occasionally reaching out with a wing hand to manipulate a three-dimensional image.

One struthiform stood out among the rest. His face had been reshaped, much of it artificial with matte-black patches of machinery. Synthetic leg, and prosthetic fingers on his wing hand whined as he moved. "Devlin!" he chirped, actually using his own vocal cords to call my name.

"He makes your name-sound," the struthiform next to me muttered. "But he refuses to learn those of his own feather-kind."

"Don't be offended," I whispered as Shriek left his fellow struthiforms to approach me. "He is deeply traumatized. He believes to learn someone's name will only lead to loss."

"It is against my will that a creature as mentally unbalanced as he practices medicine," the struthiform said. "But at least it is not on our own kind."

"A pleasure to meet you, too," I said, my grin at seeing Shriek fading.

"I've been learning more human biology," Shriek said enthusiastically. "I did not realize you could not keep yourselves clean without help of special materials. I will stop trying to cancel your shipments of head-feather-cleaning supplies."

"*You're* the one messing up the shampoo rations," I groaned.

Shriek shook out a wing hand. "I've learned a great deal of specifics about human biology studying here. I'll be a better surgeon for your kind now. Let's not hover overlong, looking at the past, arguing about such petty things as who canceled shampoos," he said.

I was entirely planning to throw him under the bus when we got back to the platoon's quarters. Everyone had been griping about shampoo for weeks.

"Have you met the Pcholem yet?" Shriek asked, abruptly shifting conversational direction. "You should, you are famous. It would be delighted to meet someone exceptional."

"I've never seen Pcholem before," I said. "Where is the pilot?"

Shriek spread his wing hands wide, knocking me back. "You are an ignorant hatchling. Pcholem are not pilots; they are the ships themselves."

Shriek began leading me upward.

"Imagine a seed born in space, unfurling its wings to feel the solar wind. Do you know there's a turtle in a zoo in one of your cities that the Accordance took over management of? It's two hundred years old!"

"That's a jump in topics," I pointed out. "I don't see your point."

"There's the elephant and a fly," Shriek continued. "The fly is tiny, it lives a single day. Very fast, quick in life. One single spin of your blue globe. And then, the great, larger elephant. It lives for decades of your solar years. Around and around the sun. And trees, well, there are trees that are thousands of years old. Great big slow things, they last longer. Do you follow me?"

"No, not really. Shriek, we're getting up to the surface. You need armor. Why the hell aren't you clad? You know the rule: Rockhoppers never—"

"You fear death, hatchling. Good for you. I died all those years ago when I watched the Conglomeration burn my planet. So imagine that seed I told you about stretches its newborn wings wide and soaks up light. It chews up dust from the nebulous vacuum around it, growing the natural biological fusion reactors deep inside its midnight-black skin. And it grows, ponderous and large. And it lasts and lasts, my human."

I nervously checked the air as we walked through two airlock doors held open, a breach that should have led to a lot of rushing air and drama. I decided to leave my helmet down, recessed into the back of my armor.

"Where do they come from?" I asked.

"Where do they come from? We do not know. Maybe they don't come from anywhere. Maybe they are always swimming around. But we know when they're born, their souls are entangled on the quantum level, just like our secure communications equipment in our armor. They're always splitting souls, budding new ones."

Shriek walked out onto the surface of Titan, and all around us a shimmering curtain held back the hydrocarbon atmosphere. We were under the belly of the ship. The Pcholem itself.

"The Pcholem don't just live for hundreds, maybe thousands of years. They won't say. But they travel between the stars with time dilation. So, they have seen civilizations rise and fall, wars gutter out. And always they keep swimming between the stars. Long after I finally admit to death, long after you wither, human, this Pcholem will eat the dark between the stars."

With that said, Shriek waved at the dark, curving belly above us. He walked toward a black tongue of a ramp ahead of us, and the darkness at the end of it.

"This is a war we are in. But even in the mud, and death, and shit, and blood, there is beauty, Devlin. Take a moment to come with me and meet a being that may have been navigating the depths of space before your species could even rub two sticks together."

We stepped onto the ramp. "Are we supposed to be going aboard?" I asked, looking back. There was no security, no Accordance telling me to get back to where I belonged. Just the dark maw ahead.

"No one tells Pcholem what to do. They ask for a favor," Shriek said, marching on ahead of me with purpose. "That seed I told you about, once it grows, the older Pcholem gather around it and bless it with upgrades. Like the nano-ink on your friend, or the armor around you. And with those grafts, it gets the ability to extend itself. They grow, change, adapt, as they find things they want or when they find new technologies that they value and will trade for more things to bolt onto themselves. They'll come down into a gravity well, though they hate it here."

"And this one, it shuttles supplies around for the Arvani?"

Shriek whistled. A derisive sound. "It decided to do this. To bring more supplies here to help Shangri-La. It must have its reasons to pull itself into such a small package of only a mile long, to slim its fields down until all we see is the core."

We walked into the darkness and stopped.

A second later, a green glow suffused the air around us. The gothic arches and swoops of the interior loomed with ghastly shadows.

Then the darkness around us faded away, the walls

becoming translucent. Outside, carapoids continued plodding to unload cargo alongside other human contractors.

"I apologize," a voice said from the darkness above, echoing smoothly around us. "The last time you stood here, you flew from a burning world."

"Hello, Starswept," Shriek said.

"You know its name." I was shocked. Shriek refused to learn names.

"It is one of four in this system," Shriek said. "I think it has come down here because it is smart. They value life above all else. Particularly their own, for they are ancient and each life is a precious thing. They are down here to help the Accordance, to help humans. They'll move us around like pieces on a checkerboard. Supply the pieces. But they won't fight."

"They are pacifists," I said.

"Of a sort," Shriek said. "Corner one, and it will do anything it can to live. But it avoids that corner at most costs."

"Then why are they part of the Accordance?" I asked loudly. "Why live under Arvani bootheels?"

The answer came from the halls of the living ship as Starswept replied. "You have seen the Conglomeration's evil. And Shriek has seen it as well, from this very spot. Is that not a will worth frustrating?"

Something was coming down a hallway toward them in the dark. The green light finally glanced on the body of a carapoid, again with those strange carvings on its carapace. "I hear," Starswept said from around us, "that you humans miss your own food, so the last time I was on Earth, I made a point of acquiring something for you."

The carapoid's thorny arms broke free of the powerful armored wings to hand me a wicker basket filled with boxes of chocolates.

“I’m told,” the Pcholem said, “that this is an appropriate gift between your kind. Is that so?”

I held the basket as delicately as I could between my powered alien-alloy fingers, trying not to break it. “It is.”

“I asked Shriek to bring you here,” the Pcholem said. “You killed the Conglomerate abomination that flew to the lunar satellite of your home world. This is a pure act. An act that Pcholem do not forget. We seek to see all such abominations the Conglomeration has made for interstellar travel destroyed. Know this: You are known among Pcholem, Devlin Hart!”

“I—okay,” I said, stumbling over words. This was getting weird.

In my earpiece, Amira’s voice suddenly kicked in. “Devlin, I need you to get out here. Now. I found something.”

4

I left Shriek holding a basket of chocolate, with orders to get it back to the platoon barracks. Ancient alien ship from beyond the stars or not, Amira finding something meant shit hitting the fan.

Rifle in hand, riding a hopper out that I'd commandeered to bus me out with a grumpy-as-hell pilot, I headed out for her location.

"You're not going to like it," she said. "Foster's going to shit."

"Why?"

"I'm way off base. I'm into Accordance zones of control. The nearest base is Needlepoint, one of the humans-not-allowed places. It's a jurisdictional mess."

"What'd you find?"

"A weak spot in Conglomeration shielding. A buzz. A small bit of leakage. A mistake. But it's under the rock. I got them. I fucking got them. They're here."

"You make the call to HQ?"

There was a pause. "Rubbed their fucking noses in it," Amira said, no small amount of satisfaction in her voice.

"Then phoned in to Accordance channels I'm not even supposed to know exist and gave them coordinates. There is a lot of traffic coming my way."

Even as we flared out over her positions, with the two squads ringing her, I could see even more vehicles converging on us in the sky.

My earpiece started pinging. My helmet filled up with notes from HQ.

Foster was shitting bricks. Accordance too.

I jumped out of the hopper when it was still thirty feet up, cracking the ground underneath me as I landed. Somewhere underneath the rock was something. Something Conglomerate.

Nearby, Accordance forms dropped to the ground as well. The beetle-like forms of several carapoids trundled toward us, massive energy cannons held in their spiky wing hands. Behind them, two squid-like Arvani officers in full armor scuttled over the ground toward us. Their legs kicked up ground-up pebbles in their haste.

I grimaced as they approached.

"Fucking told you so," Amira said on the common channel to everyone arriving.

The Accordance information specialists called it ghost sign. The trace of Conglomerate systems somewhere out there, hidden away. Hinting at the presence of something else on Titan with us.

In the common room, hours later, shucked down and out of armor, Amira held up a cup of a fruit juice and gave a rare celebratory shout. The nano-ink tattoos on her cheeks glinted in the bio-light, and her eyes fluoresced. "They may have kicked us off the site," she said. "But at least they're aware."

I placed the basket of chocolates on a coffee table. I pushed one of the boxes toward Suqi. "No tasteless alien food engineered merely to deliver a balanced nutrient mix for human consumption tonight," I said. This was a party. Or as close as we got in the CPF when deployed.

Suqi lit up. "Is that real chocolate?"

"Help yourself."

"I'm sorry to drag you all out with me for so long," Amira said to everyone. "Consider the juice a thank-you."

One of the new platoon members, Patel, held up his paper cup of fruit punch. "How the hell did you get this?"

Amira smiled. "Don't ask me."

"But seriously, this is real," Patel said, awed.

Amira gave him a blank look, the smile gone. "What'd I say?" She looked around at the new platoon members. "Newbies. I swear, no one say shit, or I'll break fingers."

Patel laughed, but Ken shook his head. "She's not kidding."

The smiles died away and the celebratory mood with it.

Ken raised his cup. "Captain Foster is still angry. We are going to be cleaning toilets for weeks, Rockhoppers. My only regret is that we do not have something alcoholic to put in these drinks."

I nodded. Ken hadn't been the one to get the calls from Foster. And the next morning, I had a meeting. To face HQ anger in all its glory. "Something to make the juice kick, yes," I said. "We could have used Boris."

Ken slumped a little bit. "Yes," he said quietly. I had to lean forward to hear him. "Boris would have figured out how to brew something or smuggle it in."

Even the veteran Rockhoppers glanced at each other, not sure who Boris was.

Ken shook his head and tossed back the fruit juice. "I'm going to turn in," he said softly.

Amira walked over to me and jammed an elbow into my side. "What the hell is wrong with you?" she asked.

"I didn't think it would hit him that hard," I whispered.

"Don't talk about Boris around him yet. He's not ready for that."

"I'm sorry." I looked down at my empty paper cup. This was turning into a dud of a party.

"Also, quit staring at Suqi Kimmirut," Amira said, her voice even lower. "That would really fuck up morale. You're not going to climb the CPF chain of command effectively that way."

I did my best to look outraged. "Since when are you all rules and regs?"

"Look, we don't shit where we eat." Amira's eyes flashed silver and black over her brown cheeks.

"That's crude," I protested.

"Doesn't make it less true."

I changed the subject. "You did good out there. With the Accordance really paying attention, maybe they'll find something instead of it finding them."

"Welcome to the real war," Amira said. "Still think I'm too obsessed with hunting for Conglomerate ghosts?"

"Do you think I'd be happy about getting my face chewed off by HQ if I didn't believe you?" I said.

"Thank you for doing your job, *Lieutenant*." Amira rolled her eyes. But she grabbed my paper cup and refilled it. As close to a thanks as I would ever really get.

And good enough for me.

Lights out, which meant smacking my shins into the bunk bed in the tiny room next to the common area. My armor loomed by the head, Ken's by the foot, and Ken stirred when I hit the double bunks. "Sorry," I whispered.

To accommodate the new squads, we'd shifted things around, gotten more cramped. Lots of doubled bunks. I'd given up my quarters to one of the new squads and moved into a room with Ken and Amira until we could get some extra rooms for the platoon.

Ken started softly snoring again, back to sleep after my jolting the bed.

I could hear Amira hitting her own bunk. As I lay down and looked up at the metal bars above my face, I thought about her CPF chain-of-command jab. Did she think I was a lifer? I raised the triangle-and-globe tattoo of the CPF on my forearm into the air and squinted in the relative dark at it.

The thing was something I didn't want burned into me. I was here because the Conglomeration was worse, because I'd seen them kill on the moon. I'd seen their tools at work in the skies of Saturn.

I hadn't talked to my parents since the war started. I wondered what they thought of their son, the Accordance hero. The last time I heard about them, one of the CPF intelligence officers, Colonel Anais, had told me they'd joined an Earth First group demanding that humans not fight the Conglomeration until the Accordance offered independence.

I could see why they believed that. They hadn't seen the Conglomeration burn through one of *their* friends. The pilot, Alexis, wasn't going to be memorialized by them. They'd never seen a cloud of crickets darken the sky.

Never would, if I could do anything to stop it.

But that wasn't going to stop them from trying to do something crazy back on Earth.

I rubbed my face. I hated this moment. Lying here, waiting to fall asleep, while my brain began to spin and spin.

At least the wind wasn't howling outside, like it had been on Saturn. The refinery we'd taken had never let us sleep due to that constant howl of wind. Left us jumpy, exhausted, making mistakes.

This bed was pleasant.

I looked up at my armor. Almost close enough to reach out and touch. Ammo and rifle at its feet. A guardian knight, recharging itself with its chest open wide and waiting for me to slam on in, looking over me in my sleep.

I never felt safe unless I could see it as I lay still, waiting for sleep. Waiting for the drift.

Amira started to snore.

A thudding sound. Armor moving around. I rolled out of bed. "Who's that?"

Ken sat up, groggy. "What?"

Someone screamed. I jackknifed out of the bed and out to the door. In the bio-light, I saw a figure stagger forward. "Chef!" I yelled, recognizing Berkhardt. "Report."

Berkhardt raised his handgun and pointed it at me. I froze, suddenly unable to move. I'd been fighting with Berkhardt since Titan. Since what felt like forever.

The utterly too-loud crack of a shot slammed through the corridor and Berkhardt's brains blew out the front of his temple.

"Chef!" I couldn't help myself.

One of the new members, Maria Lukin, stood behind Berkhardt's body as it fell forward and hit the ground with a wet thump. Her hands were shaking as she lowered the handgun held in both hands to steady the shot.

Then she moved forward as something slithered off Berkhardt's back. Oily, scales, and pronged rear feet that scrabbled at the floor as it ran down the corridor toward Lukin. The pink tail whipped around for balance.

Lukin fired twice, the corridor lighting up. I flinched each time. The driver flopped to its side.

Her face was pale in the dark. "They said in training he's already dead," she said to me. "They said he's already dead, right?"

I unfroze. "Get in your armor!" I shouted. "Now!"

Maria rabbited away, and I realized that was the first thing I should have done. Rockhopper rules. What the hell was I thinking?

I spun back into the room and started backing into my armor. It wrapped itself shut around me, and there was the suddenly cool sensation of something slithering up my tailbone and neck. The suit linked itself directly to my brain.

"What the fuck were you doing naked out there?" Ken shouted.

I willed the helmet to pop up, and it slid up and over my head and slammed in tight.

I looked left. Amira was in.

"Rockhoppers, armor up!" I shouted, using the suit to amplify my voice. It was quavering. I hoped no one noticed. Chef had been staring right at me in the corridor, I thought. Chef had his brains blown out by *one of us*. That look on Maria Lukin's face. I couldn't shake it. "Don't do anything but fucking armor up!"

The public channel was packed with scared chatter.

Ken calmly cut through the noise. "Quiet, all! Ping me if you're armored and armed and then stay in your room and make sure no one's naked."

"Are we under attack?" Amira asked.

"There was a driver," I told her and Ken on the command channel. The armored suits used quantum-entangled communications among the officers. The enemy wouldn't be able to overhear anything here. "It got Chef. Lukin shot it. Him first. Then it."

"Chef?" Ken sounded shaken.

"She shot him, and then she shot it. Twice," I repeated tonelessly. "Be ready for anything."

"I don't hear anything about orbital defenses being breached," Amira said. "HQ is silent."

"Let's get out there and find out what's happening," Ken hissed.

Amira had her EPC-1 slung over her back. A rocket launcher–looking tube with high-density battery running around every bit of spare space and cabling running down the back. The electromagnetic pulse it created stopped Crickets dead cold. Would have been useful on the flight back to Shangri-La.

I looked out into the dark corridors, thinking back to Icarus Base and all the corpses we'd walked through back there. "Alpha squad, Sergeant Berkhardt isn't with us. Smalley, you're squad leader."

Lana Smalley. I could imagine her biting her lip as she processed that. Then a calm "Understood. Chaka, Zizi?"

"We heard," they said.

"Let's poke our heads out and take a look around," I said.

5

Alpha squad was down its sergeant. But as we followed protocols and poured out of the tunnels and up toward the surface, a quick roll call revealed that no one else had gotten hit by a driver. Min Zhao had Bravo assembled and sweeping clear ahead of us. Erica Li, Jun Chen, and Greg Vorhis all had stations along the walls and zones of fire covered.

The new additions clustered in the common room. Charlie and Delta hadn't done any night raid drills yet.

"Okay, our role is to protect one of the smaller artillery positions up on the hill," Ken explained to them. "We're going to head out across the basin. We don't know what's up there, so focus on getting to the rally point."

"Alpha takes lead," I said. "Bravo on the rear. Yusef, you take our left flank, Tony, our right. Follow our pips and stay calm."

There was a ton of general chatter going on. Squads trying to figure out leadership on the open ground above us.

"Devlin, you able to get to HQ and check in?" Ken asked.

I was pinging but getting nothing back. "No," I said. "Command's gone silent. Amira?"

“I’m crawling the network, but it’s chaos back there. If I know something, you’ll know it.”

“Good.”

“You think heading for the turret’s the best idea?” Ken asked.

“Fall back on orders, assess, and then make a call. If they need us to be there and we aren’t . . .”

“Rockhoppers,” Smalley called out on the common. “We’re moving.”

“You think this is it?” Ken asked me as the platoon moved up the tunnel, Amira overriding the airlocks and blowing the air out so we could just run through and out onto the plain.

I looked through the night gloom with the armor’s amped-up senses. The giant seed-shaped lump of the Pcholem at the center of the basin blocked most of my field of view, though I could see other squads popping up out of the ground.

We’d come out looking for a fight. And it wasn’t here. And it didn’t seem about to drop on our heads, either. No matter how I scanned the sky, it came back dead. Though anything that could fly was scrambling up into the air and getting clear of the base.

“You think they’re coming for Titan?” I asked. “I don’t see anything in the air that isn’t ours.”

“Not yet,” Ken said with conviction. “But they’re coming.”

I looked around. Nothing but CPF. And scoured rock. “Get on the artillery. Keep them together.”

“Where are you going?” Ken asked. I was beginning to split off from the platoon.

“HQ,” I told him.

“Don’t go alone,” Ken said.

I slowed. “Charlie squad, on me. Delta, you’re responsible for both flanks; stay in the middle and look both ways before crossing the street, got it? Everyone, keep alert for human hostiles."

There was a pause.

"Human?" someone asked.

"You saw what happened to Chef. I don't think he'll be the last, if this is something serious."

Several bodies lay scattered around the tunnel entrance to HQ. Torn apart. Shot. Blood splattered on the walls. We slowed down as we approached, rifles up, nerves amped as we expected every shadow to jump at us.

A suit of armor lay facedown in one of the airlocks we cycled through. Tendrils of smoke leaked from around the shattered helmet.

"Direct RPG hit?" Patel asked.

Kimmirut leaned over. "No blast marks on the outside."

"Eyes up," I ordered, stepping over.

A bullet smacked into my armor, making it ring inside. I flattened back against the bulkhead of the airlock. Just before I'd ducked back, I'd seen a mess of desks piled up against the HQ entrance in a hasty barricade.

"Hello, the shooter," I called out over the speakers on the suit.

"Oh, thank god!" came the immediate response. "Is everyone else there with you able to talk?"

"No drivers here," I said. "Can we step out and approach?" I put my armored hands out in the air.

"Please! We need help putting out the fires."

We vaulted the barricade, bouncing off the ceiling and coming down into the middle of a mess. Fires raged in three parts of the round command center, and the offices were all already gutted. Five people fought, but the smoke kept them back. Their CPF grays were charred at the arms. One of them had nasty burns on her hands.

"Get the extinguishers from them and get into the middle of the fires. Yank out anything on fire and toss it down the north tunnel," I ordered. "Clear the barricade."

"There might be more attacks . . ."

"The fire will kill you now, attacks might come later. We can make a new one," I said. "Why are you shucked down?"

"We were off duty," the woman with the burned hands said. She was trembling. Shock hitting her. Those hands looked bad. "The drivers hit officers' rooms. There were a lot of officers out here. They cut us off, so we got handguns and retreated back here. Two of us got into armor, but the drivers . . . they can still get their tails through. All we could do was retreat to here and call for help, but it was already on fire. We decided to try and hold it."

I'd changed rooms. Given a squad my room. That driver in our hallway, it had been hunting me.

Damn.

"We just lost all our leadership in one strike," I said. "Anyone have a first aid kit?"

Someone was hunched over at one of the boards, trying to call out. Good thinking. "Anything?"

"Needlepoint's quiet," he said. "I'm trying to figure out how to call up to orbit, but I'm not a comms specialist. I'm trying to figure out the interface."

Mohamed Cisse had flipped his helmet up and pulled me aside. "The woman with the burned hands needs a medical pod."

"We're all staying right here for now, I'm sorry," I said. This was all fucked up. I wanted to rub my forehead. "Get your helmet back up; we don't know what's happening."

"Yes sir."

"Hey, I made contact with the ship!" the man on comms yelled.

I strode over. "The Pcholem?"

"Yeah. What do I tell it?"

"Tell it to leave. We're under attack." If there truly were only four of them in the entire solar system, like Shriek had mentioned, then it was a big sitting duck.

"Cancel that!" Someone in an armored suit with commander's stripes on the shoulder walked down the tunnels at us. "We might need an evac."

"Sir," I said. I started to give an update, but the commander ignored me and pushed aside the person at comms.

The armored helmet snicked down. The commander had her hair pulled back in a ponytail that bobbed as she looked over. "Needlepoint has an automated call for general assistance going out," she said, eyes flicking over the screen. "But all the satellites are up, all orbital defenses and weapons ready, and no breaches have been detected. I'm going to get a line up for instructions."

Gunfire started chattering from a level below us.

The commander's head snapped over to the HQ entrances leading downward. One of the fires inside still burned merrily, but Charlie squad had stomped, extinguished, and ripped out the other two. Her lips pressed tight, she twisted my way and I could see the name on her collar: CHARET. "It's coming up from below," she said. We'd been so focused on being hit from above. But the ghost sign that Amira found had been underground. "Deploy your team *that* way."

She pointed down, but I was already on it. "Charlie squad, we want to block the doors coming in from below."

"What about the fire?" Yusef asked.

"Now!" I shouted. "I want weapons on those two doors!"

+ + + +

The next wave came. Hollow-eyed people running up the corridor at us. The Driven never spoke, but they had weapons. They used them. The hasty barricades of desks we shoved up toward the inner doors shattered under the onslaught of fire.

There were too many. They just kept coming. Bodies, the drivers clutching their shoulders with clawed hands and blood running down the fronts of their shirts.

"I'm out of ammo," a shaken Patel said.

"Punch anything that comes over the barricade," I told him.

Underneath us was an entire complex of contractors. The tens of thousands of civilians who slept assuming we were defending them.

"They waited for the next round of command talent to organize here," Commander Charet said. She had left comms and walked up behind us. She held a duffel bag, which she tossed forward. "I thought I was going to have to blow the airlocks leading out, not the ones leading down."

Patel grabbed the bag. "I've been trained to set explosives," he said.

"Let's give him cover," Charet ordered, and flipped her helmet down.

A driver scrambled up and over the barricade and launched. I fired reflexively at it, trying to pick it out of the air. But it landed right on the back of someone's armor. They flailed around, and the pink tail whipped up, and then down and in. Wriggling micro-tendrils sliding through normally impenetrable alloy until it reached skin. "Yusef!" Suqi screamed, running at him.

He hit her, throwing her back several feet. His helmet slid open and Yusef, eyes wide, coughed blood. He grabbed a grenade off his waist, pulled the pin, and jammed it down his neck, and then his helmet snapped into place and he crouched down.

There was a thud. His armor bowed out from the inside. The helmet cracked open and Yusef Obari fell forward onto the ground, smoke rising from the inside of the husk of his armor.

"Holy fuck."

I could hear the sound of retching on the common channel.

"Patel!" I shouted. "Move!" If we waited any longer, we'd be run over.

Patel was over the barricade with the bag of explosives. Everyone opened up, picking off each body that tried to sprint its way across the corridor down to us. For several minutes, there was only calm breathing and gunshots. No one had to say anything.

Patel didn't even wait to get all the way back to us before hitting the remote detonator now in his hands. The explosion blew him through the barricade, knocked us all on our backs, and left me with a nosebleed.

"Charlie squad, call out."

"Kimmirut here."

"Patel," Patel groaned.

"Cisse."

There was a lot of smoke. I swapped a few different filters over the helmet until I could peer through the smoke and see the way down choked in rubble. "That should hold them a while," I said, my voice breaking slightly. I looked down. My armored hands shook, and I couldn't force them to stop.

Commander Charet grabbed my shoulder and spoke on the common channel. "Patel, is there enough to do a repeat?"

"Yes," he said, staggering to his feet and shoving a heavy desk off of him.

“Anyone not in armor here in HQ can’t go outside. So, you take your squad and get out,” she ordered. “We’ll stay here, keep calling for backup, and get the assholes in orbit to see about lending us a hand. I’ll also see if I can link up with any soldiers stationed downstairs who’re not being Driven.”

“You sure about that?” I asked. “We can keep your guard.”

“Protect your team, Lieutenant,” she said. “Get to the hills, and watch your feet.”

“What about yours?”

She snorted bitterly. “I was taking a shit. Can you believe that? Pants down around my ankles when I heard the screaming. Officers’ quarters. I get there, anyone not in armor, they’re just bloodstains on the wall. This private’s running around in armor, killing anything in sight, driver swinging from his back. Two shots. He goes down and it slithers off his back, but not before hitting me.”

“In full armor?”

“Four broken ribs. I’ve been coughing blood, my left arm doesn’t work, and there’s pain in my abdomen. Only reason I could walk over here was because I jammed myself full of painkillers and let the armor walk me. See where things stand? Get with your platoon, hold the hills, wait for orbital support to get down.”

We loped across the Shangri-La basin as the explosion died away behind us, sealing them into HQ.

“Amira, status?”

“Nice of you to check in. We’re locked in; what’s the state of HQ?”

I filled her in as we ran.

“Holy shit,” she said.

"I know!"

"No, I'm looking out over the basin. You need to run faster. They're coming out of the tunnels into the open now."

A figure in armor lurched toward us. Suqi Kimmirut slowed down, pulled out a rocket launcher she hadn't been able to use inside, and hit it midstride, knocking it back in a ball of fire.

"Don't slow down!" I shouted. Then back on my platoon command channel. "Amira, that gun we're protecting. Can we turn it around to face down into the basin?"

"I like it. We need more manpower."

"Then start recruiting," I ordered.

We hit the foothills. I dared a glance back and saw people only in surface suits, no armor, stumbling out into Titan's atmosphere, compelled by the creatures dug into their backs. They fired weapons randomly. A wasteful wave of humanity tossed against anyone trying to get away.

"Crickets," Mohamed Cisse shouted. A cloud of the small Conglomerate mechanical insects blew out of one of the tunnels near the Pcholem and boiled across the ground toward the Pcholem's open bays.

"Well," a voice said over the common channel. The Pcholem, Starswept, sounded very apologetic. "I'm very sorry to have to do this, but there is heavy Conglomerate weaponry coming online. I must take my leave. I wish you all the best of luck in your current battle."

The living starship hauled itself into the air, fields compressing down around it as the gloom filled with a sudden onslaught of fire and weaponry aimed against the Pcholem. Crickets and human beings slid off in the air to fall down to the ground as Starswept accelerated away.

We were on our own.

6

The basin floor crawled with a flood of human forms and scrabbling Crickets balling up to attack positions in the foothills. Ken perched on a rock to look downslope. "Crickets and drivers," he said. "I'm not seeing any trolls or raptors."

"Yet," I said.

"Yet," Ken agreed. We watched a wave of Conglomeration surge against the lower slopes. Second Platoon struggled to keep them at bay, falling back in careful staggered lines with well-coordinated fire.

"They're rushing us, Amira." I turned back to where Amira, the rest of the platoon, and fifteen other soldiers pulled in from the hilltops were slowly shoving the anti-spacecraft energy weapon into place. It wasn't mounted; Amira had to have it moved onto a large cairn of boulders and rocks hastily built for it.

Barricades at HQ. Rock piles. We were stretching.

Soldiers were pushing up the rear of the barrel and stacking rocks under the cannon's stand to get the weapon aimed down into the basin.

"We have three covering the tunnel," Ken said. "We can't risk blowing the cable down."

"So, we're vulnerable on the hill and from below."

"Just from below now," Amira said. She walked over to stand with us and raised a hand. "Fire!"

The energy cannon fired, a subsonic thud. The air around the tip rippled; energy lanced out. A line of blinding light jumped out to hit the basin. Five at the back were moving the barrel around as Amira started calling out targets.

A halfhearted response came in gunfire. Then a small wave of Crickets swarmed toward the hill. Amira stopped calling out directions and pulled out the EPC-1. Massive clumps of Crickets tumbled to a stop after she fired; the rest veered off and wheeled back toward Shangri-La's tunnels.

Cheers came over the common channel.

"They can still kill the dark matter reactor down there." Amira slung the EPC-1 back over her shoulder.

"And we don't have much in the way of ammo, other than what we carried up here," Ken said.

"We just need to give the folk upstairs enough time to drop reinforcements," I said.

"If the reactor goes offline?" Amira asked on the command channel.

I let out a deep breath. "I don't know."

"Now is the time to figure rally points," Ken said.

"Where?" I asked through gritted teeth. "If they're boiling up out of the ground, where do we go? How do we know where to go? We leave this spot, we walk into what?"

"We sit here and fight to the last?" Amira's voice dripped scorn. "You know my feelings about that crap. I'm here to survive. I'm not here to throw my life away to either the Accordance or the Conglomeration."

I opened my mouth but was cut off by a familiar voice. "Third Platoon, this is Commander Barbera Charet."

Relief washed over me. "HQ, go for Third."

"Upstairs has marching orders, Lieutenant," Charet said. "I need you and your team to detonate the weapons foundry and hold the power plant until the ships get down here."

I looked up at the cannon. "Right now we're holding a hill and directing fire down—"

"I know. That's why I'm choosing you. The foundry has a few bombs big enough to destroy access to it; you'll know what to do." Charet coughed and went silent for a second.

"How long will it take for backup to arrive?" I asked.

Silence.

"HQ?"

The sound of gunfire cracked the channel open. An explosion. "I'm going to have to get back to you," Charet said.

"HQ? HQ? Commander Charet?"

I looked over at Ken and Amira. "We have orders," I said on the common channel. "Charlie, Alpha, you're going to split off with me. We're headed down to take the reactor and hold it until help arrives from upstairs."

"HQ just went down," Amira said up on the command channel.

"And we have orders. We hold the reactor, we can hold the hills. You know, Amira, the only way off this planet is up. Ken, Delta and Bravo stay with you. Keep sweeping the basin."

"There's a good chance anyone going down there dies," Amira said. "It's crawling with Conglomerate forces."

"I've been there before. It makes sense, Amira."

Amira walked over to the tunnel and looked down. "You're going to need someone who can open doors and hold your hand. Also, you don't want to go down this tunnel."

"Why not?"

"They're waiting for you there. They won't be waiting for you somewhere else in the middle of the basin."

I wasn't going to ask or order her. I knew her position. "Okay. We're going downhill. Alpha takes point. Charlie covers our asses."

"You need me to open doors," Amira repeated.

"Let's go, Rockhoppers," I said, with a calmness I didn't feel in any way. And beside me, leaping up over the hilltop and down with us, was Amira.

"Thank you," I said on the command channel.

"I'm thinking, before we blow up the foundry, I want to pick up some more weapons," she said.

We boogied down the tunnel after unleashing lightning from the hilltop along our chosen path to force everything well back. Charred bodies lay around the basin as we pelted down into it, hopping and bouncing our way along.

Amira came in behind us, hitting even higher and longer jumps into the air and firing her EPC-1. She left a swathe of twitching Crickets on the ground.

"Left," I ordered.

We veered and hit the inside of a loading bay, preceded by a hailstorm of our own bullets before we dropped in.

"Amira?"

"I'm worming my way into the networks. No ghost sign."

Good. This was the old routine. The first routine, really. Amira had used all that black-market Accordance nano-ink technology buried under her skin to look around corners, check out surveillance video.

The doors opened and we scooted through. Under Amira's

guidance, we began moving through bulkheads and doors, section by section. One squad would provide cover while the other moved. Then we switched places. Doors opened under Amira's thoughtful pauses, and then we'd keep going.

Left, right, down, someone with a driver on their back attacking us. Kill. Crickets, stomp and kill. Drivers, open fire.

We spent five minutes jammed up near the foundry as one of the Driven came at us in full armor. But we'd known it was there, thanks to Amira.

Amira came around the corner with the EPC-1 and hit the armor, and then ducked out. Zizi Dimka hit it with an RPG, and Chaka sniped the driver right in the head halfway down to the ground.

Amira walked into the foundry and looked around. "Grab all the extra ammo you can stand to carry," she said to everyone. "Level up to something with more punch if you need it. Devlin, the bombs are for jumpships. They will need to be dragged out to this bulkhead, and the next one. Should bury it enough."

Charlie squad sat on the bulkhead doors, covering our asses as we set up. Amira tripped the timers, and then we hoofed it down the corridors again, moving down through the basin's warrens.

The bodies in the corridors weren't soldiers anymore. They were contractors in overalls or simple day clothes. A cross section of humanity, lifted out from different continents with the promise of work and a chance to help keep humanity safe.

Here on Titan, we didn't see all the anti-Conglomeration videos. Having seen battle, we didn't need it. But in downtime, the platoon had uploaded some of what Earth was seeing. The Conglomeration's work on other worlds: stripping them of life and keeping only the forms and genetic material that interested them. The Conglomeration had needs, niches that could be filled, and it would take life and reshape it, mold it, to fit any of those needs.

On the moon, we'd seen living heat shields that lived on the outside of a Conglomerate starship. They'd once been a thinking, intelligent race like ours.

I wondered if these people had come here out of a desire to fight, to help the war effort. Or if they'd been starving in refugee camps run by the Accordance and saw no other way out.

Gunfire. We hit the walls and skidded to stops.

"We're CPF," I called out on the common. "Identify yourself."

"How do we know you're CPF?" came the reply.

"Because we didn't try to kill you," Amira said irritably, and walked around the bulkhead out into the open. She flicked her helmet open. "Now—"

Someone shot at her, the single pop loud and bright in the tight space.

Amira moved, blurringly fast. She grabbed someone in blue overalls and pulled a handgun out of their hand. "I'm going to say that you're having a bad day and a little over-nervous," she said. "That is why I have not killed you. But I am obviously not Conglomerate."

She tossed him back toward a group of people in lab coats, overalls, and day clothes. Behind them were heavy blast windows, control rooms, miles of complex alien machinery plunging down into the ground. Gantries and crosswalks laced the air above the reactor pit.

One of the engineers in an environment suit stepped forward. "Apologies," he said. "We're trying to hold the reactor."

Amira held the handgun out to him. "This should be yours. Who are you?"

"Anton Dismont; I'm one of the chief engineers," he said,

and then waved the gun away. "I'm afraid I'm more likely to kill one of you by accident with that than help. Are you here to save us?"

Amira looked back at me. "Alas," she said. "We've been sent here to help secure the reactor until help arrives."

Dismount slumped a little. "We're still under attack."

"Very much so. For now," I said. Then on the command channel: "Amira, can you get me a big boost on the common so I can get a message out to everyone?"

"Thinking of replacing HQ?"

"Yes. We have the power plant. Now let's start securing the base."

Amira raised an eyebrow.

I gave the mental command, and my helmet snapped open and slid into the back of my armor. "If we have the plant, then the hills are secure. Get me on the common channel, Amira."

I couldn't tell if she shrugged, but her silvered eyes looked upward, as if she was recalling something. "You're live, Lieutenant."

Ignoring her slight mocking tone, I said, "All platoons, this is Devlin Hart. We have the power plant secured. The hills are still ours, even though the Conglomeration has taken the tunnels. But now it's time take back Shangri-La.

"I need volunteer squads to get down here. It will be door by door, but we have a systems specialist that you can coordinate with. Let's flush them the hell back to wherever they came from!"

Amira broke out of her trance, mind running deep inside Shangri-La's networks.

"How many?" I asked.

"Three thousand got into the hills," she said wearily. "Platoons agreed to send down a thousand to try and secure the tunnels."

"And?"

"I got them in," she said. "Staggered opening doors to let them clear through by sections. Most of the cable tunnels are secure. A few hundred are fanning out from those points. They're breaking back into HQ, but it's heavy with drivers and raptors there. And that's about as far as we can go right now. And, Devlin?"

"Yeah?"

"Stop pacing. You're in armor. You're making the engineers nervous."

I stopped and looked around. The civilians were staring at me.

"We need more boots in the tunnels," I said.

"The other officers won't," Amira said. "They want the hills covered. A way out."

"Well, we get HQ back at least," I muttered. "But we can pull this all back."

The sound of gunfire interrupted me. I moved up toward the doors and glanced up the tunnel at Lana Smalley. "Smiley?"

"Clear!"

I stomped back to Amira. "HQ? Anyone alive?"

She smiled. "They found only bodies. They're holding it now, though."

For now.

This was all a balancing act that could go horribly wrong so quickly, I realized. And it would take days, or weeks, to clear everything out down here.

But it was possible.

It was damn possible.

"HQ incoming," Amira said.

"Who's taken command?" I asked.

"The officers are still in the hills. Privates who volunteered to push through," she said. "They have a link upstairs. They're saying other bases are scattering to the plains; they're managing to get uplinks and orbital bombardment support."

"Are we expected to abandon the base as well?" I asked.

"No. If we can hold, we are to stay put. However, other officers on the plains and some Accordance chatter are rumoring something big is up from everyone upstairs."

"Like what?" I asked.

"It's fucking alien high command," Amira said. "They're not going to tell us 'apes,' are they?"

7

Ken popped back into the command channel. "We can't call down orbital strikes on Shangri-La itself; they won't engage until we're out in the open and headed for rally points."

I looked over at Amira. "But HQ is still telling us to stay put?"

She'd been glazed over, off in a world of networks to help coordinate clearing out the tunnels for hours. She looked exhausted.

"Amira?"

"We're still staying put," she said, an edge to her voice. "But raptors are running around everywhere, and everyone's starting to run low on ammunition. We shouldn't have blown the foundry."

"We had orders," I muttered.

Amira didn't bother to respond.

Min Zhao's voice came in on the command channel. The four squad leaders had been keeping quiet, leaving most of the chatter to Amira, Ken, and me. They stayed on their squad's entangled comms mostly. "Everyone, we have a very large breakout that is coming up the foothills."

"How bad?"

“Thirty or forty raptors in armor, a couple drivers, big cloud of crickets,” she reported.

“Are you in danger?” I asked.

“They’re going after First Platoon. They might have to abandon their spot. But that’s not why I’m calling in.”

I cocked my head. “What’s up, Max?”

“They’re being led by an Arvani in armor,” she said. “And it’s broadcasting on the common. You should hear this.”

“Amira, you hearing this?” I asked.

“I’m hunting for the signal,” she said. And then the sound kicked on for me.

“Do not resist the Conglomeration,” a familiar voice said. “You have lost on all the other worlds you fought for. You will lose here as well. The Conglomeration is stronger than you or the Accordance. But if you surrender now, walk away from your positions, you will have a place in the Conglomeration. A great place. You won’t have to live under the pressure of the Accordance’s grip. You will have freedom. You can have self-determination. You can have riches.”

“That Arvani . . . ,” Ken said.

“There is a further bounty, however, for those willing to prove their true allegiance to the new order that comes to this world. A promotion to high status, and the natural benefits that will stick to you with this. The bounty I will give to anyone who hands over the following three humans here: Devlin Hart, Amira Singh, and Ken Awojobi.”

“Seems like you’ve got a fan,” Zhao said.

“I killed your kind in great schools on the moon of your homeworld,” the voice continued. “I will kill all that oppose me here.”

Amira blinked right out of her trance and we stared at each other. “It’s Zeus,” we both said.

"Zeus?" Lana Smalley asked. "The defector from Icarus Base? That Arvani is dead, along with all the other Conglomeration there."

"Obviously not," Amira said.

"It could be just some other Arvani who went over to the Conglomeration?" Min suggested.

"With a personal vendetta. No. It's Zeus." I was sure of it.

"First Platoon is falling back, they can't hold. We lost the gun."

"This is HQ on the common," came an interruption. "Pickup is coming. Pickup is coming. Get down into the basin, hold off any enemy, and get aboard."

"They're abandoning HQ now," Amira said. "They just don't have the ammo to hold off the raptors in the tunnels. Everyone is running topside."

I wanted to punch something. If we'd been able to dig out the foundry, get more ammo . . . maybe. Amira saw what I was thinking and shook her head.

"Ken, keep on the gun as long as you can to hit anything Conglomerate out on the basin."

"Until the guns are blown, they'll need power," I said. Gunfire chattered from up the tunnel again as Alpha and Charlie stopped something in its tracks that was coming at us. "And there are civilians down here, we'll need to escort them up."

"It's going to be a zoo up there," Amira said.

"I know." I looked around at the unarmored engineers in their bright-yellow plastic-looking vacuum suits and rubbed my forehead. "I know."

Two hilltop anti-spacecraft weapons had been seized by several humans with drivers on their backs, protected by five raptors. They spat lines of energy into the sky, lancing around at the jumpships weaving around to try to get into the basin.

Out in the basin, a flood of yellow vacuum suits and civilians rushed the wasp-like ships the moment they touched ground. There were drivers leaping into the mess, shoving tails down into spines and spinning the civilians around to their own purposes, only to be executed by soldiers in armor.

Raptors boiled out of the tunnels, and CPF soldiers hanging out of the sides of the jumpships opened fire on them.

Several squads stayed on their hills, raking the basin with energy. The scarred rock bubbled and boiled, dead Conglomeration obliterated.

Then the hilltop guns stuttered out and stopped firing.

At least that would let more ships get to ground. But now the basin was a scrum.

"There is not enough transport for the civilians," Ken said as the platoon re-formed in a rough circle near one of the larger jumpships.

"Holy shit," I said, looking at the numbers of people surging around the basin to try to get aboard anything that was flying. "This is a disaster."

"It's happening all over Titan. The Accordance wants soldiers back. It wants to preserve fighting strength. The civilians are extraneous to them," Amira said. "You know they do not value human life."

Over and over on the common channel, pilots were shouting, "Spaces are reserved for armored and fighting personnel first."

Despite that, CPF soldiers were shoving civilians into ships and guarding the basin, expecting them to fly away and come back. Or at least, refusing to jump in first.

"Keep the perimeter," I ordered the entire platoon on the

common channel. "Anyone who wants to get aboard, can. But I'm going to stay right here until they bring down more ships."

"Think hard about that," Amira said on the command channel, her words clipped.

"No," I said. "We're in armor. Hundreds of pounds of protection and enhancement. Three or four days of air. Water. Nutrition dripped right into our bloodstreams. Adaptive camo. We can get out there into the plains and survive for a pickup. Everyone standing out here in yellow is a target. That's time for us to figure out what to do next, time these people will never be able to get for themselves."

Amira shifted on her feet visibly. I could sense the coiled frustration even through the armor. "I don't like this," she said.

"No one is *supposed* to like it," I snapped. "That's why I told you to get aboard if you wanted. I'm not going to stop you. I told you what I'm doing, anyone who wants in can join. I can't force you to do this, particularly when it's against Accordance orders."

"Don't shout at me," she said calmly.

I was freaking out a bit. Because I knew they would all probably follow me out into the plains. Into a giant gamble that we would get picked up later, even if the Conglomeration was overrunning the base.

But this *was* the right thing to do.

"There were so many we never got a chance to save back in Icarus Base," Ken said, surprising me by interrupting us. "Devlin's right. We have time to come up with another solution. They don't. I don't want that on me. Not again."

Thank you, Ken, I mouthed to myself. Thank you.

"I'm not—"

"They're taking off!" someone shouted on the common

channel. The jumpship we'd been guarding powered up. Pebbles and rocks slapped against my armor and rattled as it rose into the air.

A handful of yellow vacuum suits staggered back to their feet and looked up as their way off Titan accelerated out over the hills.

All around the basin, more jumpships rose, scattering to the points of the compass gently and then picking up speed.

"There they go!" said a voice on the common channel. Zeus. "Your heroes. Your leaders. Your soldiers. The Accordance. They've left you all behind. Now what? I will tell you. Now you will learn what it is like to live as true, free humans."

"He's coming downhill," Ken said.

I could see the distant cloud Zeus and his team of raptors were kicking up as they raced down into the basin. A mile and a half away from us in the center of it all.

"Surrender now," Zeus shouted on the common channel. "Sit down with your hands folded and you will live to see a new day for your species. You will learn how the Conglomeration extends its welcome, even to its most bitter enemies like my own species. But remain standing and I *will* cut through you."

"Always a charmer," Amira said.

An engineer in yellow tapped my armor. "What do we do now?" Dismont asked. I could see condensation beading the inside of his mask.

"You all have two choices," I said. "Sit down and surrender, or run with us out into the plains. I don't know how long your air will last."

"What happens if we surrender? We've seen the videos the Accordance plays. But you're CPF. You've been on Saturn. What happens to us?"

All we knew were the same Accordance pieces of propaganda.

Dead planets. The Conglomeration's reshaping entire species into functional forms for their own needs. But we didn't know what happened to the people they captured and ruled over.

The communications from places that fell went silent.

"I don't know," I said. "I truly don't know."

"Then we go with you," Dismont said firmly.

I looked at the dust cloud of the approaching Conglomeration force. "That's assuming we can even get out of here," I said.

8

We grabbed ammo from squads who were sitting down and folding their arms. "No judgments," I shouted. "Just grab what you can."

Zeus was a mile away now, and the slow picking through surrendering people meant we weren't moving away quickly enough. But I wanted everything we could get our hands on.

"Are we sure none of the ships are coming back down for us?" Tony Chin asked.

"If they were only taking soldiers, something bad might be going down upstairs," Amira said. "I've been trying to patch in, but there's a lot of interference. That can't be a good sign. . . ."

One of the skyscraper-sized anti-orbital guns glowed red. Electricity sparked up its sides, gathering into a house-sized ball at the very tip, and then leapt into the sky.

"I think shit's all fucked up and shit," Lana Smalley said.

"Has anyone seen Shriek?" I asked. He would be able to provide some hints as to what might be happening. He'd seen more of this than any of us.

"He got on the jumpship," Ken said.

"Of course he did," I said.

"We need to move," Amira said. "Not many people standing anymore. We stick out."

"Where are we going?" Dismont asked.

A good question. "If the jumpships aren't coming back down, and everything is up in the air—" I started.

"Not everything," Ken said.

"Can anyone here repair a broken jumpship?" I asked on the common channel.

One of the yellow vacuum suits in our midst raised a hand. "I've worked maintenance before getting promoted down to the power core and retrained. What's broken?"

"We sucked crickets into an engine and then crashed," Ken told him.

"We'll need parts," the engineer said.

"Amira? Where can we find parts?" I asked.

We were all moving as a group, trying to keep the yellow-suited engineers in our midst. Amira broke away for a tunnel. "Downstairs," she said.

After the heavy doors shut behind us, they groaned and started smoking. "What's that about?"

"Slowing Zeus down," Amira said.

We had to make the hard choice of loading up with spare engine parts instead of ammo. We left the guns on the floor. But with a plan at hand, the four squads pulled together quietly.

Mohamed Cisse carried a turbofan on his back like Atlas, the engineers clustered near him, and we formed up around them. Amira led us back up and out. We popped out like groundhogs and ran for the hills. After a few lopes, we started dropping even more gear and just picking up the engineers under our arms so we could leap our way from rock to rock.

A triangular formation of raptors fell in behind us, but Ken took Alpha squad and fell behind a bit. The firefight was intense and brief.

We crested the hills and pelted downhill toward the open plains and the ethane lake where we'd crashed with the new platoon members just a day before.

"Keep up the pace," Ken muttered. "We went down a long way from the base, and the engineers don't have that much air. Don't stop for any Conglomeration, just keep moving."

I didn't respond. I was too busy focusing on each armor-enhanced leap that took us farther away from Shangri-La.

"I think the Conglomeration may be taking orbit," Amira said, looking up from the bank of the ethane lake.

I looked up as well. But there was nothing more than Titan's usual gloom and thick clouds. "How can you tell?"

"I'm listening hard. Through the static. I think I'm feeling some battle chatter. Ship-to-ship stuff."

Three squads got their shoulders under the jumpship and lifted it up. "I think I just shorted something out," Erica Li said. "Someone take my place."

They all staggered the jumpship up out of the liquid ethane, letting it all gush out of the gaps as they waited, and then carried it up onto the bank.

Someone started coughing on the common channel. "Shit, same here, something blew inside my suit. There's smoke."

"Contact," Ken said.

"Take Alpha and engage," I said. "Bravo, Delta, circle up

and keep the ship in the middle. Charlie, you're there to help the engineers move anything heavy."

As everyone scrambled to, I stood by the jumpship and looked out across the ethane lake, half expecting crickets to come boiling out of it again. But there was only stillness.

A moment of calm in the storm. It caught in the back of my throat, like a hiccup. As if I'd still been moving forward and then suddenly braked, and everything came up.

The sound of weapons fire floated over Titan's air, breaking the moment of stillness.

"Ken?" I asked.

"Raptors. Scout team. We've been located," he reported.

"Fall back and tighten up. Charlie, you'll have to help the engineers and shoot anything that gets through. How is the ship looking? How long do we need?"

"Two hours," came the response.

"We have fifteen or twenty minutes before the bad guys hit us," I told them. "Hurry."

The first wave of crickets hit ten minutes later.

The next hour, we ground the crickets down as they came at us. Amira took point, using the EPC-1 to down them in swathes. Anything that got through, we stomped into tiny debris.

But the raptors that came in afterward required bullets and direct confrontation, though some of the mines that Ken had taken the time to lay down killed many in the first batch. There was no running now. We had to keep them from the jumpship as the engineers swore and removed this part and that part.

It didn't take long to run low on ammo, even despite short

bursts and frequent direct confrontation. It took three to four of us to wrestle down a single raptor and break its helmet or shove a grenade into some key part of the Conglomerate armor.

We were losing people. Several engineers dropped in the crossfire. Aran Patel started screaming when Mohamed Cisse jumped out and caught a raptor that leapt into the inner circle. It had swung around and ripped open his armor with the wicked nano-filament blades on its legs. In seconds, Cisse ended up shredded, and his armor scattered around the ground before everyone opened up.

"Out," Min Zhao shouted.

And more and more of the platoon started tossing weapons to the ground.

The sound of a loud belch got me to stare back at the jumpship, as I'd almost forgotten what it was we were doing here.

"Everyone get in," Amira yelled. "I've got power."

"You're flying it?"

"No one else can interface with the systems or has any experience."

We fell back. Charlie squad covered us from the doorway, which now was just Aran Patel and Suqi Kimmirut.

There were too many of us. We crammed into the jumpship face to face.

"Amira?" I asked.

The jumpship's engines leapt up an octave, trying to push us into the air. Instead, we scraped along the rocky ground. Metal screamed and something snapped off the bottom of the jumpship.

Energy beams sliced against the sides of the ship, one of them punching through. Blood and flesh splattered against my helmet. The ship bounced off a boulder, spun slightly, and smacked into something. I wiped blood away just in time to see a yellow vacuum suit spin out of one of the large rents in the side of the jumpship.

"Hold on!" Amira shouted. The jumpship wobbled higher into the air and the ground started to fall away. "I think I'm getting this."

The jumpship shuddered again as we rose slightly higher. Another loud bang from something striking the side made me jump.

Alarms started whooping from the cockpit. "We going to make it?" I asked.

"I'll get back to you on that," Amira said.

9

Saturn filled the sky, massive and roiling with clouds, the rings casting shadows over the clouds we'd struggled to get above.

"I'm getting comms," Amira said. The jumpships had direct quantum entangled linkups into the Accordance. But the minds on the other side of a call could be halfway across the solar system. Getting answers about what was happening overhead, and convincing them she was for real, had been taking up her time as we continued to spiral farther and farther up toward the clouds.

"I can fly the ship. But I don't know anything about getting a craft like this to orbit," Amira had said when I'd asked her why she was spending so much time trying to call in rather than getting us the hell upstairs.

And the engineers only had rough guesses about how orbital dynamics worked. As they pointed out, we didn't want to run out of fuel trying this. Or end up in the wrong place.

"Okay," Amira said on the command channel. "I've explained

our situation and sent back our fuel levels and dynamics, and Accordance is on the other side talking me through our sequence. It's tricky."

Tricky. It must have been if Amira was happily chatting with Accordance pilots over comms. She was not the type to stop and ask for help.

"There's a ticking clock. The ships in orbit are getting ready to punch out and leave. We have a very limited window to get scooped up in time. We don't have enough fuel to come back down."

"You're saying we may get stranded in orbit," Ken said.

"If we make it, yes," Amira said. The jumpship banked to the right. Yellow and brown clouds far under us appeared through the gaps in the ship's hull, and the wind screamed through the cabin as airflow changed. The entire jumpship flexed and warped.

Swearing cluttered the common channel as everyone tensed, waiting for the jumpship to rip itself apart.

"Amira?"

"Fuck, I know," she said, sounding rattled. "I'm trying to line us up. I'm doing the best I can, but the software is struggling with all the damage and I'm not a pilot; I have no idea how much we can push this. So, we might not make it up. And there might not be anyone there when we get there. But I know I can get us back down to ground."

I was sure the rip in the hull near me had gotten wider. "We should ask on the common channel."

"Oh, really, Lieutenant, it's suddenly a democracy in here after all those orders you've given out of late?"

"I gave everyone an option at the jumpships on the ground, and I notice you stayed. That was your choice," I said.

Amira grunted. "You two idiots would have killed yourselves

down there without me. After all we've been through, you're the closest thing I have to family."

"Sergeant Singh, are you getting all sentimental on me?" I asked. One of the other squad leaders snorted and tried to smother it.

"I've had to carry your asses so much, I feel like a mother duck," Amira said. Then on the common channel: "Hey, everyone, I need you to make a choice: up or down." She outlined the situation as she began to point the jumpship slightly up, gaining more altitude.

There was silence for a while.

"That's a hard call to make," someone said.

"You have ten seconds to aye or nay it," Amira said. "Then our launch window closes."

With a loud shriek, a panel ripped away from the top of the jumpship. I looked up toward the purple darkness of space above us. It looked like an electrical storm far overhead, with lightning dancing from spot to spot in the vacuum up there. It lit up gas clouds, like miniature nebula.

Then one of the tiny dots lit up, the explosion slowly expanding. A ship exploding. I realized the clouds were debris, all backdropped by the massive bulk of Saturn looming over us all, making our life-or-death battles seem insignificant.

"Three, two," Amira said.

"Punch it!" I shouted. "Go, go!"

The jumpship tilted slightly higher and the Accordance-made engines kicked on hard. People clattered around the cabin as a whirlwind kicked up inside. Everything shook hard enough to blur vision. Some started repeating a phrase in a language I didn't recognize, but I knew what they were doing: praying.

After a few terrifying minutes of acceleration, the jumpship rolled over onto its back. An engineer screamed and someone tried to grab at them, and then they were sucked clear out of a new gap in the ship's frame. The yellow figure kicked and wiggled in the air as they fell away behind us.

We were riding the skeleton of a ship to orbit.

The engines kicked out. Titan's clouds passed far underneath us and the curve of the planet-like moon could be seen on the horizon.

"We're still alive," Min Zhao marveled.

"Amira?"

"Shut up and don't talk to me. Orbit mechanics *suck*." The jumpship spun around and the engines fired up, nudging us back down toward the clouds a bit. Then it shifted again, pointing forward and firing. Amira was constantly changing orbit.

Occasionally, Amira would swear.

The entire horizon lit up, something white-hot blazing away. It started to move, gathering speed, and then faded off into the dark. Then another blinding spot did the same.

"Carriers making a run for it," Ken said.

"Hold on," Amira said. "They're coming for us."

"I don't see anything." I looked out the numerous holes in the jumpship around us.

"There we go," Tony Chin said from closer to the front.

Something slipped across the darkness between us and Saturn. Inky blackness slipped off its skin.

"That ours?" I asked.

"Uh-huh," Amira said.

The darkness opened its mouth and revealed a cargo bay full of other jumpships inside. It was moving faster than I realized. "Oh, shit!"

The lip of the cargo bay slammed into the jumpship, which spun all the way around until the back end struck the deck and halted the spin. The ship bounced across the bay, smacking into pillars, and came to a stop up against the back wall of the bay.

Four struthiforms in full armor bounced up to the side of the jumpship and ripped the doors off. "Get out!" they ordered.

The docking bay was closing up like a large mouth after swallowing, Titan disappearing behind it.

Accordance lights began to strobe and flash.

"Launch is imminent. Secure yourselves!" The struthiforms scattered and bolted for safety.

A deep thrum vibrated through the Accordance carrier. Then it launched. Anyone not holding onto something was shoved back to the wall. A damaged jumpship farther up the bay groaned, its tie-downs snapped by our ship on the way in.

"Watch out!" Ken shouted.

The carrier accelerated harder still, gravity pressing down on all of us. The jumpship slid down the bay and slammed into three of the team in armor.

"Everyone okay?" I shouted. "Who got pinned?"

Before they could answer, a beam of light sliced through the cargo bay, burying itself deep in the ship. Everything shuddered, but the carrier kept moving. But now the entire side had been sliced away, and we were all staring out into space. Staring at the beams of light searching and stabbing for us and the other carriers.

We watched the winking lights and explosions of the battle we were accelerating away from and held on tight.

10

We built an impromptu camp at the corner of one of the sealed bays after the acceleration eased and the alarms cut out. Struthiform crew in harness uniforms came by with crude cots.

A veritable cross section of Accordance subjects crowded in around us. Struthiform soldiers in their own powered armor, carapoids lying along the back wall like large lumps of polished rock, and other humans with their gear.

One recognizable struthiform approached us, his scarred and half-machine face blinking at the bright, stadium-like lighting in the docking bay. "I heard your approach to the ship."

Lilly Taylor jumped up. She'd shucked her armor. It was behind her, splayed open like something hungry and half machine, half biological, waiting to eat her again. The bright lights seemed to get soaked up by her skin as she went for Shriek's throat. "You bastard!" She'd spoken before with a more precise, almost British accent. Now I could hear the Kenyan accent coming out with her anger.

Min Zhao was on her feet, grabbing Taylor and spinning her off to the side.

Shriek seemed neither surprised nor concerned, regarding them both with his dinner-plate eyes.

I was on my feet too, leaving my armor behind to back Zhao up. "Thank you, Max."

"Maria is gone. We died trying to get up here. Trying to *save* these civilians," Taylor shouted.

Zhao wrapped Taylor up in a bear hug. "He's an alien, Taylor. We're alien to him. He's a lost soul and he's not going to look at it the same. But he still fixes us up, don't forget that. Okay?"

Taylor crumpled for a moment in Zhao's embrace.

Shriek looked back at me. "This is why I do not learn names," he said coolly. "They die. Now I know the dead one was named Maria. What good is that now for me?"

I groaned. "Fuck, Shriek, now's not the time."

"It's good that she grieves. You should all grieve. Grieve now and let each other go," the cyborg struthiform said. He pointed toward one of the large high-definition displays on the bulkhead wall over our heads. "See that small dot there? The blue one? That is your world. Your Earth. I would find a place on this ship, or wherever we end up, to go and look at it one last time. Because the Conglomeration comes for it, and they'll burn it. And then, eventually, you too."

I pulled Shriek away from the platoon. Alpha and Bravo were used to this shit and just looked annoyed. But Charlie and Delta were ready to kill the medic.

We needed a medic.

"I'm half ready to kill you myself, Shriek," I said, out of earshot. "You might be an alien, but right now you're being a real asshole. Shut up about all that. Did you find Ken?"

"As you requested," Shriek said. "He was shot. It happened on the surface, but he didn't report it to you. His armor kept him stable but was compromised. I assume he didn't want you to worry about taking him into pure vacuum."

I let out a deep breath. "Let me go armor up and we'll go look at him."

"The armor stays in the bay," Shriek said. "Ship rules."

"Rockhoppers don't shuck," I said.

"You're on an Accordance carrier accelerating away from the field of battle," Shriek said. "If you want me to take you to see Ken Awojobi, you shall leave your armor, like any other person who wishes to walk the ship."

I bit my lip. "I'll get Amira."

Ken was cocooned in a medical pod, its spider-like arms tucked neatly away. He sat up as he saw us, pulling coconut-like fibers sinking into the skin on his back out to their limit. "I'm sorry," he said.

"For what?" I shook my head. "Shut up, I don't want to hear about that. I'm just glad you're okay. When you stopped responding, and we didn't know where in the bay you were, we didn't know . . ."

"How is everything?" Ken asked. "How bad? I saw the whole side of the ship get sliced off."

"Maria Lukin, one of the new soldiers," I told him. "She was over there. She saved my life in the corridor, back on Titan. Shot Chef when the driver took him. Shook her up. She was a quick thinker."

There was nowhere to sit. Apparently, aliens didn't expect bedside visitors. Amira folded her arms. "How you feeling?"

Ken nodded. "Better. I'm pretty drugged up. We'll see

when I get released how I really feel, because right now it is warm and very fuzzy, which doesn't feel right. We just barely got out alive. It doesn't even feel real to be sitting here, to be still."

"Barely alive," I agreed. "I think I believed that when the Accordance handed us some resources and weapons, we'd get in there and show them how fucking hard we could fight. I thought, maybe they just didn't have the warrior spirit. Weren't motivated enough. But that was a nightmare. We lost Saturn, and now Titan, too. What's it going to be like when they reach Earth?"

"I get that from Shriek," Ken growled. "I don't want to hear it from you, too. Listen to me: I didn't almost die for nothing just now. We didn't fight for nothing. We're going to go back to Titan. We're going to go back and kick their asses, and I'm going to be first on the ground. Because the Accordance is not going to roll over and surrender. The Accordance is better than that. They are strong. We are lucky they are our allies."

There was no food for humans aboard the carrier. By the end of the second day, the engineers were lying down and taking sleeping pills that Shriek offered them, while the rest of us armored up. The steady nutrient drip jacked into our spines was enough to stave off the worst, but it was strange to just mill around in full armor, conserving power and waiting.

Halfway through the third day, the monitors lit up with something other than the outer ship cameras.

A series of rocky asteroids connected by clear tubes and girders flashed on screen. "These are the Trojans," a familiar voice explained. "These asteroids trail along Saturn in its orbit, and serve as something of a naval yard for our Saturn operations and a rally point for Accordance ships engaged on the Saturn Front."

The asteroid base faded away, and a familiar face appeared on the screen with the triangular CPF logo up behind him.

"It's Colonel Anais," Amira muttered, with all the enthusiasm of someone who found dogshit on the heel of a shoe.

"Here at the Trojan naval base, we will begin preparations to defend against any incursion into trans-Jovian Accordance territory," Anais said. "Your valued participation in the wars around Saturn has helped reduce Conglomeration forces. You have struck a great blow. Now please gather yourselves for the next stage."

"What about Titan?" someone shouted, as if Anais could hear them. "We just leave them all there to die?"

Anais droned on more about future plans and the bravery of the CPF.

"We left a lot of people behind," I muttered to Ken, now recovered and suited up. "What are we doing here? We should be going back to save them."

"We're surviving," Amira said. "We're still here. We can't help them."

"Apparently," Ken said bitterly. The news that we weren't going back to Titan seemed to have shaken him. His previous bravado had faded away as the drugs left his system. But I was still surprised. Ken had joined the CPF to get into the officer corps. He'd wanted this. Badly. He'd been a full believer. In the Accordance, in our role in it.

Looking over at the remains of Charlie and Delta squads, and the tired faces of my platoon, I realized Titan had left us all broken.

11

After several days crammed into a docking bay, filling it with the stench of human and the acrid odor of struthiforms and carapoids, the platoon was moved out from the carrier and into the rock of one the Trojans.

We were close to the surface. On the second day, one of the walls blew out and sucked half a dozen people away.

The Rockhopper's "no shucking" rule became ironclad. We walked around in armor or huddled together in the carved-out end of a tunnel.

"Millions of miles through outer space, kitted with cutting-edge weapons, and we're sleeping in a cave," Ken noted.

Seven plastic buckets spaced out around our spot captured water dripping slowly, like honey, from a broken pipeline over our heads. Accordance had installed a gravity plate somewhere so we could walk around the asteroid, but it was a third of Earth's gravity. And it was strung through the center of the rock, which meant weird things happened if you turned your neck too quickly or turned a corner.

All night long we lay and listened to the drip, drop, drip.

A few miners came by on the second day with a large auger and some baffles. They'd drilled through the rock, breaking out into the vacuum. As the air whistled away, they calmly installed the baffles, sealant, and then a simple plastic box over the hole.

"We now have an outhouse," Ken pronounced in disbelief.

In full armor, we joined the morning mess call, surrounded by humans covered in dirt finishing their drill shifts. They looked exhausted, haggard. More like zombies than real people.

I remembered on the moon seeing Earth First slogans and general anti-Accordance graffiti.

These people didn't have the energy.

"These conditions are inhumane," Ken muttered.

Amira raised an eyebrow. "You've never heard of the Paris work camps? LA?"

"Those are for terrorists," Ken said. "Agitators."

"This is the Accordance," Amira said. "Half the people on my block were hauled away to work in worse places than this. This is a fucking hotel, Ken."

"They created infrastructure in my country when no one else would bet on us," Ken said. "They changed everything. The way things were before they came? My parents would have died. Of hunger. Or disease. The Accordance did many things for humanity; it's just that the little slice of a percent that stood on the backs of others before the Pacification are upset they are no longer Earth's royalty."

I stood up with a ball of Accordance human-optimized feed in one hand, and a globule of water in the other. Since the retreat, with nothing to do, they'd been circling around each other. Amira, raised on the streets that fought back against occupation, black market nano-ink proudly marking her as hostile, criminal, to the Accordance. Ken, raised by his family to be a part of the officer corps working for the Accordance.

Maybe our friendship had only been that of three people stuck in a foxhole together, trying to survive.

Now we were living in a cave that dripped, shitting into outer space, and eating Accordance glop while we waited for . . .

. . . I wasn't sure what I was waiting for.

Min Zhao waited for me as I got back to our cave and shucked out of the armor. When I stepped out, my paper underclothes soaked and stained with sweat, she said, "We need to figure out how to divide the squads. Charlie . . ."

"Not now, Max. I just need to sit and eat my human kibble."

I sat on my cot and nibbled at the tasteless ball of gray playdough.

Zhao shot me a look, and I sighed. "Seriously, Zhao, leave me the fuck alone."

Looking hurt, she nodded curtly and retreated back down the cave.

Shriek came to find us a few days later, once we'd fallen into a schedule of clomping over to the meals and then getting back to our cave. We cleaned it up as best we could, but we were jockeying against every other soldier among a variety of species stuck in the warrens inside the asteroids the Accordance had pulled together to make the yard.

We were still showering with wet napkins and flushing them out the crude space toilet. Welcome to the Trojan point, where clumps of asteroids followed the majestic ringed planet around in the same orbit. And humans flushed their waste and trash out into the same trailing orbit.

"What are we waiting for?" Ken had asked, and no one had an answer for him.

The Accordance had us in storage for now. We'd been saved from Titan, and now we weren't needed as the spaces on the board got rearranged.

"You need to take advantage of this time," Shriek said. "I can give Amira directions to the human holds. There are places to drink, eat, and enjoy the company of the other humans here. You are no longer on the front wing of the attack, and you need to realize this."

"We've been fighting for a long time, Shriek. You don't need to lecture us," I said.

"You barely survived a full evacuation. You need to spin about in the wind and realize that, just for now, being alive is its own amazing moment," the struthiform said. "Because if you do not, what was the point of trying so hard to stay alive."

"Ostrich ET's gotta point," Amira said.

"Alright, armor up," I said. "We'll go over, check things out."

"No armor," Shriek said.

"Rockhoppers don't shuck," I said.

"Then you stay here, in this damp cave, by yourselves. Well done, humans, you have made staying alive as exciting as a scabby infection."

But I knew with certainty that leaving armor meant leaving us vulnerable. "Bravo, Charlie, Amira, Ken. Let's go investigate."

Groans floated through the cave.

"Tomorrow we switch," I said. "We need people standing by the armor. We will not leave it alone."

Shriek clicked approvingly and led us off through the tunnels and warrens of the asteroid. "This will be good, my little adopted humans," he said happily. "Follow along, follow along."

I was counting the turns back.

Just in case.

Our party came out of the tunnels into a large cavern filled with shanty structures made of leftover plastic panels, recycled paper partitions, all of it rigged with lights clamped onto angular, leaning structures.

People stared out suspiciously from behind peepholes, while in the makeshift alleyways the sound of chatter bounced around.

Due to the low gravity, some of the buildings looked like kids' experimental popsicle-stick buildings. Stories high and bundled together by twine. Yet standing.

Shriek led us through the dense clusters of leaning buildings and into the first floor of a wicker dome with a neon sign that blazed the name from the apex: THE PARLIAMENT.

Inside, where it was hazy due to the light gravity, low-circulating air, and total lack of carbon dioxide scrubbers, people crammed up against tables and the bar.

"What do they serve?" Amira asked. "More Accordance gloop?"

"No," Shriek said. "Rocket fuel."

"What?"

"Or," Shriek said, "more like station-adjustment fuel. I believe there are rockets that use forms of alcohol. Someone, somewhere, managed to confuse the purchase ordering forms for rocket fuel and get alcohol delivered instead. Then the humans handling the loading diverted it."

"How is it that the alien in our platoon figured out where the bar was?" Ken asked.

"When you know you are going to die, you spend time seeking out finer moments," Shriek explained.

"Shriek, shut up," I said. "Before you undo all the goodwill."

Amira looked around the whole bar. "We don't have much to trade."

Shriek swept a wing hand toward the bar at the very center, a circular table filled with humans shifting to and from it. "I have opened a tab for the platoon under my auspices."

Zhao grabbed Shriek's half-metal, half-struthiform head in two hands and kissed the top of the wrinkled, ruined skin. "I've always liked this feathered freak. Haven't I always said I love him?"

"You have never said such a thing," the alien medic protested.

"Oh, well, remember that Min Zhao says she loves you. *Min Zhao!* Come on, Shriek, say my name!"

Shriek shoved her away with an angry hiss.

Aran Patel and Suqi Kimmirut stared at us as we laughed. "Serves the fucking walking chicken right for ditching us," Greg Vorhis muttered from behind Zhao.

"Shriek doesn't want to learn our names," I explained to Suqi. "It upsets him."

"I think," Amira said, gently shoving at us, "we should get to the bar before Shriek changes his fickle little mind about that bar tab."

I managed a seat next to Suqi and listened to the back-and-forth chatter. Aran and Suqi didn't join in, but they took to the simple glasses of clear alcohol quickly enough.

It numbed. It burned. Did what it needed to do. And maybe, if we kept going, we could leave Titan somewhere behind us.

Live for the moment, Shriek had told me. Because that moment is all you'll get.

Five glasses later, I was light-headed enough to realize I'd been carrying something on my back. An invisible weight that melted away, glass by glass.

Suqi was asking something.

"What?" I asked.

"Are you okay?"

I'd been staring at her, I realized. "I'm sorry," I said. I reached out and touched her knee. Shriek was right. You only ever had that minor moment. The now. The now was all we had. Because there was nothing but an uncertain haze in the future.

Suqi's drawn-in breath jolted me. She yanked backward and stood up from the stool. "Sir . . ." She sounded embarrassed and wounded.

Yeah. Half her squad had died in front of her and someone who outranked her had just grabbed her knee.

"Shit, Kimmirut," I mumbled. "I'm sorry."

She shook her head and put the glass down. "I'm going back," she said.

I stood up to follow her and wobbled. "Ah, fuck."

I'd never been a hard partier. My parents had been more concerned with dragging me from tent camps and basements to protests. They organized walkouts and strikes, and there was no time for me to be stupid. Not when you were the Harts' son.

Here I was, playing soldier. Pretending to be a hard-drinking veteran when I was just lucky to have escaped.

But it had been a nice few minutes. The alcohol burning out chains that held me to each of these individuals. Leader. I wasn't a leader, I realized as I stumbled toward Ken. I wasn't raised to be one. Or taught. I'd just lived through a Conglomerate attack on the moon, and the Accordance used me as propaganda.

All I'd done was survive.

I tried to grab Ken's shoulder. To tell him. But Amira

intercepted me and slipped under my shoulder to steady me. "You don't look so good; let's get you back to the bar to lean on."

"You were right," I told her. "I fucked up."

"Come over here and tell me about it."

I twisted back around. Ken was in deep conversation with a monstrously tall man who had muscles on his muscles. The kind you handed the big guns to. "Ken has made a friend."

"It's been hard for him since Boris," Amira said, pushing me back to the bar. "I think he needs to connect. Maybe let off some steam. After all we went through, we all need to let off some steam."

I looked at Amira and then back to Ken. "He's gay?"

"You didn't know?"

I shook my head.

"Devlin. Fuck. You don't pay close attention to the people you lead, do you?" Amira handed me another glass of the clear stuff.

"I didn't ask for it," I said. "Any of it."

"Yet here we are."

I squinted at her. "If we all need to let off steam, have you?"

"Day we docked." Amira sipped at the glass. She didn't say it with satisfaction or relish. There was a sudden grimness to her.

"Do you feel better?" I asked.

"I don't feel worse," she said.

A group of miners off shift had been watching them. One of them got up from his table. "You assholes are here partying," he said loudly, "while friends of mine working back on Titan are dead, you fucking collaborators."

The air in the bar buzzed and snapped with voices that sounded like a set of electrical wires dropped on each other.

Amira let go of her glass and stepped forward. "What did you say?"

The fact that she hadn't sworn left me feeling suddenly sober.

The man had a certain ropiness to him. The muscles that came from spending long hours operating heavy tools deep inside the asteroid. He was covered in a gray dust, and his green eyes seemed ghostly behind all that dust.

"You pieces of shit need to crawl back into that cave you're hiding in," the miner said. "Stay back in there and cower."

I walked over. "Hey, man, we just want to drink in peace."

"Drinks *we* got into this bar. Any of you know how hard that is? Know what's going on back on Earth while you march around for the Accordance? Food riots. Executions. They're standing on our backs for a war we didn't ask for. And here you all are, enjoying a drink on the tab of one of those damn ugly walking chickens. Bunch of fucking useless collaborators."

"Hey," I started to say. They were collaborators too, out here working for the Accordance.

Amira hit him in the chin with the heel of her hand. He stood a foot taller than her, but he went back and flopped onto the table, smacking into it and scattering glasses. She was, apparently, not interested in talking any further.

The miner's four friends launched themselves at us. I still had my hands up when I got hit in the face. I should have gone down. I was not a brawler; I'd barely struggled through training, with Ken constantly singling me out.

But something snapped in me. Trying to calm the situation was no longer an option.

And I wanted to fight. I wanted to break something.

"Dev!" Ken shouted, leaping in.

"Here."

We fell in close to each other, backs in, facing out. Amira had picked up a barstool to use as a club, and two miners were out cold on the ground.

But the rest of the bar had turned against us.

There was a brief moment where we kept formation, but then the melee set in. We were all just brawling. Punching, kicking, rolling and fighting. Just us against the world, skin on skin. In the moment.

Until carapoids broke through the walls. Before the splintered pieces of wood were done falling to the ground, we were getting thrown to the ground and zip-tied with our hands behinds our backs.

I threw up onto the ground in front of me and groaned with pain as a thick pair of carapoid boots kept me shoved against the rocky floor so hard, I waited for a rib to break.

12

The door to the industrial-sized airlock we'd been shoved into rolled open. Amira and I stood up, somewhat unsteadily, shielding our eyes from the bright light. We'd been lying on hard rock for hours in the dark.

Once my eyes adjusted, I could make out that the silhouettes were five carapoids carrying stun guns and eyeing us with their diamond-like eyes. And between them all, a familiar figure. The man who'd dragged me out of a cell and into the Colonial Protection Forces.

"Anais," I growled.

"Colonel Vincent Anais," he corrected. "The first few times we met, I was working in a consulting capacity. Since the increased human independence within the CPF, I now have rank."

"Colonel," I muttered.

"Lieutenant." He smiled. His face was more pinched since the last time I saw him. More lines around his eyes. He carried a somberness around him, now, like an invisible lead cape. "I'd like to say it's good to meet you again, but with you, it is always complicated. You owe me a favor."

Colonel Anais snapped his fingers, and one of the carapoids set a chair down on the ground. Anais straddled it and looked at us all mildly.

"A favor?" I said.

He nodded and his eyes narrowed. "A big favor. Because you're still a lieutenant. Look, I know there's a lot on your shoulders. A platoon, your parents under house arrest because the Accordance needs to keep an eye on them. But you need to remember that it isn't just the Conglomeration that has it out for you, Devlin. You have enemies elsewhere. Captain Zeus's children are very upset that you maimed their mother, and they want your head. They've been waiting for any mistake. You handed it to them. Zeus's line wants you all to live in a cell for the rest of your lives."

"Wait, their *mother*?" I asked.

Ken staggered up to join me and Amira. The full-on hangover and soreness from bruises were leaving us barely able to stand in front of Anais. "Zeus is a traitor!" Ken hissed. "We fought a *traitor* for our lives. Again on Titan."

Anais nodded. "Well, traitor Zeus may be, but Zeus was still Arvani. And Arvani expect to be treated . . . like Arvani. Do you understand?"

Ken rocked in place. "But Zeus killed almost everyone in Icarus Base."

"Mother?" I repeated.

Anais looked from Ken back to me. "Yes. Zeus is male currently. Zeus was female earlier in life. They can change their sex, it is not that shocking, there are creatures that do this on Earth as well."

Ken interrupted. "Who cares about Zeus's sex. Zeus tried to kill us. We are going to be punished for doing our duties?"

"Yes," Anais said. "Zeus's progeny have high status in Arvani command circles. But . . . the CPF is independent. The pressure rolled downhill, and I convinced Command to put you all on shit detail for the rest of the war. You'll be scrubbing toilets, digging rock, and volunteering for dangerous manual labor whenever it comes up."

"They could be traitors, too, like Zeus," Ken said. "They probably are."

Anais shook his head. "I wouldn't say anything like that out loud ever again if you enjoy being alive, Awojobi. Besides, the progeny haven't left Accordance yet. They are full Arvani still, with all the naturally superior rights that being Arvani entails."

Amira's laughter stopped Anais cold. He looked at her, visibly annoyed. She smiled back at him. "Some Accordance will always be more equal than others," she said.

"You're quoting from illegal native literature," Anais said. "Again, not a smart thing to do out loud on your part. George Orwell's books have been burned or ferreted out by virus."

Amira stopped laughing and frowned. She opened her mouth, but Anais held up a hand.

"I've stopped you from being executed or even some of the other plans suggested. You're going to be on a security detail for a while until you can be moved to one of the asteroids that are being drilled out."

"This is bullshit!" Ken snapped, angry and surprising me. Amira put a hand on his shoulder.

"You're right," Anais said. "But before you get shipped off to chip rocks, or worse, there's time. And you never know what will happen between now and then. So, keep your damn heads down. The CPF is underpowered. We need you all alive and functioning. Humanity cannot afford to lose fighters. So, don't give up yet."

Someone behind me burped and groaned.

"Earth is falling apart," Anais said, more softly. "Earth First operatives are gaining more followers. And since the Arvani are diverting military resources to fight, security on Earth is faltering. We are retreating to more secure compounds, like Antarctica or the moon."

We were CPF soldiers, embedded in the Accordance. Going where they needed. We'd gotten whispers and rumors, but this was the first time hearing what had been going on in the year since we'd left. "My parents?" I asked, leaning forward. This all started when the CPF all but kidnapped me and forced me to join.

Anais grimaced. "We don't know where your parents are."

I should have known. I grabbed the desk. "Their safety was the reason I agreed to this hell," I hissed. "I gave you your propaganda victory, the son of the famous dissidents joining the CPF and doing his duty. I played the part. And then some. What the fuck am I doing here if not saving them from Accordance 'justice'?"

My anger didn't even penetrate Anais's almost-bored facade. "You're here because you know that it keeps the Accordance from just bombing any camp they think your parents are hiding in. Because you've seen that there are worse things than Accordance oversight."

"Oversight?" Amira laughed. "Occupation."

"The Conglomeration will literally mine people for what they're worth, and then refashion them into something useful for the goals of their gestalt. You might live, but your children will end up being a biological appendage to their civilization. We've seen them do it to countless worlds. And—"

"What about my family?" Ken interrupted. "What about my brothers and sisters?"

"Your family's role in the Accordance was recognized. They've been relocated to refugee quarters at Tranquility. They're safe."

"Refugees?"

"Be grateful," Anais said. "Sections of Earth are trying to devolve into self-rule. It hasn't happened yet, but the chaos is tricky. In the meantime, I need you all to stay alive, out of trouble, and out of sight of Zeus's family. I know I'm going to need seasoned fighters. I'm telling you about your families in trust. Trust that you'll understand the larger picture. Trust that you are smart enough to know what needs to be done, and that sacrifices have to be made."

Anais stood back up from his chair.

"So, now what?" I asked.

Anais looked at the rest of the platoon clustered up behind me. "Lunch is being served. Go eat, get over your hangovers. Get cleaned up. When you get back, you'll be told where security detail is. Try not to screw up. If you're not doing what you're assigned, you stay right the hell here. You only leave this little cave when you're getting something to eat. Got it?"

"Yes," I said wearily.

Anais stared at me for a while, and I looked blankly at him. Then he nodded, turned around, and left.

"You must be laughing at me now," Ken said to me on the way back to our quarters from lunch an hour later. "To see that you were right about the cost of working with them."

"No," I shook my head. "I'm not laughing."

"It wasn't the wealth we had or my own opportunities. It was the infrastructure. The cities they helped us build. The technologies we gained. The great equalization, after so many decades of underinvestment. Knowing that, with the tools, our countries could be as great as any that had looked down at us in the past. We were never stupid; it was divide and conquer. The Europeans did it between people in the past, Accordance did the same by approaching the developing world and offering them more to sign the treaties that formalized oversight."

I grabbed Ken's shoulder. "I guess Earth First, and my parents, are not going to be welcoming either of us if we ever get back home."

Amira broke the moment as she shoved us from behind. "You weepy little shits."

"Damn, Amira, we wouldn't even be here if you hadn't thrown that punch," I shouted back at her, genuinely angry.

"I'm going to have notes in my file," Ken said.

"Really?" Amira made a face. "You knew the fight was going to happen. I just decided to get it over with and skip the posturing bullshit. None of those miners were going to talk it out and you damn well know it."

"True," Ken said. Then he smiled. "Shame you spent so much time on your ass, Devlin; we could have used the help."

"The fuck?" I was outraged. "I was first to your sides. Both of you ungrateful assholes. I should have walked right out of there and left you for the carapoids."

Amira laughed. "I'm sure your parent's nonviolent methods would have worked in a bar fight."

"We don't know if we don't try," I told her, and my outrage couldn't be maintained; I laughed. "We're all fucked. I'm laughing because I don't know what else I can do."

"I know." We walked side by side, lapsing into silence. Then I grabbed them both in a hug on each side.

Whatever happened, we were going through it all together. Even if it was shit.

Amira said in a lower voice, "When we get back, you need to divvy up the squads and make some choices. You can't keep running away from that. We lost people."

I hadn't wanted to do this. But glancing back at Kimmirut and Patel, I knew she was right. They were trailing behind us all. "Kimmirut with Delta. Patel to Alpha. And four becomes three, just like that."

"Who takes over Alpha?" Ken asked.

"Smiley," I said. Lana Smalley as Sergeant. A few months before, Smiley had been standing in a giant crater carved out of the side of a flying mining platform, frozen and staring up at the clouds above. Now she turned and ran toward problems without Ken or me saying a thing.

"I'll tell them," Ken said.

"Thank you," I whispered, unsure of my own voice suddenly.

"We got through it before," Amira said. "After Saturn."

"I got used to just the two squads. I felt like maybe we should just keep going, letting the Conglomeration kill us, until there was no one left," I said.

"No one is replacing anyone else," Amira said, figuring out exactly what was bothering me.

"I know."

I had come to understand why Shriek refused to learn names.

"Hey!" I looked around. "Where is Shriek?"

"He wasn't human, they didn't jail him. He'll be waiting for us, I'll bet," Amira said.

We were posted to a large airlock, not all that different from the one we were jailed in for what felt like a night. The asteroids here kept to a twenty-hour light cycle, Arvani preferences. Several other asteroids had no gravity and had been filled with water for Arvani officers. Some of the miners had been tasked with stocking pools with shrimp and fish.

Fresh fish sounded better than goop. We weren't going to be getting any, though. Let alone any shrimp cocktail.

On the other side of the airlock was another Pcholem. Our job was to prevent anyone from getting aboard. Or even approaching the airlock doors. But no one had. So, we basically stood in front of the doors. Four hours on, four hours off. Two squads at a time, Bravo and Delta today.

"Where is Amira?" Ken asked.

"Not here," I said.

He shot me an angry frown. "This again? We're going to get into even deeper shit if you don't figure out how to lead."

"It's bullshit, Ken." I folded my arms, my rifle slung over my back, and stared at the roof. We were helmets down, and Ken had lowered his voice so we could talk to each other without being overheard. "We're in bullshit because of other things."

"Yeah, I know that," Ken said. I unfolded my arms and stared at him. But he was looking off down the tunnel thoughtfully. "I know she'll bug out. I know what happens next to us, it is unfair. But you still have the platoon to lead, and you need to figure out how you talk to Amira in front of them or they will all take it as permission to do whatever they wish. And then where will you be?"

Shriek sidled up to us. "There's no one in the tunnel," the alien noted.

"Yeah, hasn't been for hours."

He wrapped his one good wing hand and one mechanical wing hand around each of us. He hadn't even bothered to armor up. "Then let's go in and visit."

I looked at the airlock. The inner doors were ten feet high. "No. We're here to guard it."

"How many times do you get to say 'Greetings!' to a Pcholem in a lifetime?" Shriek asked, leaning in close. "When your world is destroyed and you flee for your lives soon, you'll want to know the beings taking you to safety."

"We are already on thin ice," I said.

"I do not recognize the metaphor," Shriek said. He let go of us and started banging on the doors, his artificial wing hand banging loudly. "Hello, Pcholem! We outside wish permission to come and speak. Let us talk! It is so boring; aren't you bored?"

"Shut up!" Ken hissed. The two squads on duty were turning around and staring at us with various levels of concern.

"This is . . ." I stopped as the doors lurched aside. Air whistled for a second, popping my ears as the air pressure equalized.

I stared down the ramp toward the dark-black, coral-like structures inside. Very different from the smooth gothic arches I was expecting to find. But this was another Pcholem, not the one I'd been on down on Titan.

"Enter," said a voice.

Shriek looked back at us and half bowed with his wing hands out and then turned and started down the ramp.

"Stay on guard," Ken ordered the two squads still staring at us.

"Facing *that* way." I pointed at the tunnel into the asteroid to emphasize his order. "Shriek, get the hell back here." I started down the ramp, and Ken followed.

"This is a bad idea," he said.

"I know."

The airlock doors slowly shut behind us.

13

Green bioluminescence increased until our shadows loomed against the curved walls of the interior of the living alien starship. Our footsteps were muffled, the sound soaked up.

"Please," the Pcholem's voice said, "keep walking to find your companion. I will direct you."

The tunnel's strata shifted, down into a rocky substance. Here and there, we passed through grafted-on metal tubes. We turned as the Pcholem politely requested it. Occasionally, we walked into cathedral-like spaces that hummed with alien machinery. Carapoids looked dully at us and then went back to scurrying around.

We broke out into outer space. Startled, I sent the impulse to snap my helmet up, terrified that the ship, a creature that lived in vacuum, had led us outside by accident.

"You do not need protection," the Pcholem said gently over the common channel. "My fields extend far beyond the visible length of my hull. You are safe."

I saw that Shriek, in no armor, stood out in what looked like empty space a hundred feet away. The stars in the darkness that seemed to yawn before us.

"What should I call you?" I asked, snapping my helmet back down with a snicking sound.

"Unexpected Dust," the Pcholem said.

"May I call you Dust?" I asked.

"No. I said my designation is Unexpected Dust. If I wanted to be designated Dust, I would have told you this when you asked."

I looked at Shriek, who spread his wing hands. "Unexpected Dust is a grandfather to Starswept."

Starswept. The ship that left us on Titan. Because the Pcholem were pacifists, happy to move us around like pawns but not stick around.

I understood humans not wanting to get drawn in. But Pcholem were Accordance. An integral part. I wasn't sure what to think of them. Were they giant cowardly starships? Or just smart?

"Starswept has heard you are visiting me, and gives greetings from the orbit of your birth world," Unexpected Dust said to me.

"You can talk to Starswept?" Amira asked.

"Some time ago, the Conglomeration once bargained with us. They were deep in the gravity wells but had the hard metals and curious things we wanted," Unexpected Dust said. "They helped give us entangled, instant communication. Instead of having to swarm together to keep our minds in synch, we could scatter where we pleased."

That was surprising. We'd never heard this before. None of this was approved Accordance history. I was very interested to find out more. "You worked for the Conglomeration?" I asked.

"We do not 'work' for any species," the living starship told us. "We trade. We move individuals around. We seek mutually beneficial arrangements with anyone broadcasting on radio frequencies displaying coherence. We like to negotiate rights to gas giants in particular, so we were saddened by the loss of the ringed worlds here; they were pretty to swim in."

"But now you're Accordance, right?" I asked.

"We have begun a mutual alliance after the Recent Unpleasantness," said Unexpected Dust.

Shriek nudged me. "They live a long time; they're talking incidents that are almost a hundred years ago."

"What happened?" I asked.

"The Conglomeration happened," the ship said. "They attacked some of us, tried to breed us to create a fleet of ships they could control. But they are a fast species, short-lived. They had no patience. They created the Constructs from our living tissues and histories and technologies. We remember the Pcholem they used, our cousin. And now, whenever the Constructs appear, we can taste, smell, hear those *things* that used to be Pcholem but are not really Pcholem. Perversions. Tortured, mindless, broken and reshaped. For that, we will hate the Conglomeration until the suns fade away and die."

"Those jellyfish-looking starships," Ken said. "Those are the Constructs. They're remade Pcholem."

"Yes. The Conglomeration pollutes all it touches," the starship confirmed. "There are few Pcholem in this galaxy. We are long to mature, hard to create. Each one of us is a precious mind, a unique and ancient structure that we have carefully fashioned ourselves into. To steal something so carefully self-made, to destroy an individual, is abhorrent. For that, we will help the Accordance attack them. We will help you also, in your quest. And we are delighted to meet the humans who fought against the Conglomeration when Starswept was deep in the gravity well and vulnerable. Your gift, your losses, we do not take these lightly. You are known to the Pcholem. Know this."

A carapoid walked up to us with a small package carefully wrapped in a green bow.

"It is my understanding that humans exchange small tokens of appreciation," Unexpected Dust said. "Here is a selection of chocolates. Please enjoy them during your guard duty. Please do visit again."

The carapoid left us, and then the fields we stood on began to darken.

"I think it's time for us to leave now, Shriek," I said.

The struthiform cocked his head at me and shook himself. "Its attention is elsewhere now," he agreed.

As we moved back through the ship toward the airlock, I wondered out loud, "Unexpected Dust?"

"Think about it," Amira said.

"What?"

"You're going faster than light. What's the worst thing that can happen?"

I thought about it for a second. "Oh."

"Is that a depressing name or a bad-ass name?" Ken wondered out loud.

But neither the ship nor Shriek knew.

The airlock doors rumbled back open.

14

Bravo squad had shucked down and were taking turns behind a cheap plastic booth to scrub down with wet wipes. The corridors had gotten thick with people being shifted around, temporarily sleeping in rows near the food halls while they waited for their next orders. The air had gone from smelling like saltpeter and rock to human sweat as unwashed bodies crammed up against each other in the asteroid.

Every level was packed. And when the platoon dallied, they swapped rumors. There was going to be a push to take Titan back. They were being gathered for a retreat back to Earth, skipping right past Jupiter, the belt, and Mars.

Whatever the plans were, they were keeping us in the dark, keeping leaks down.

Ken wanted to go back, I could tell. Wanted another chance at Titan.

But maybe, I thought, beefing up Earth to protect what was most important made sense. Maybe we'd be back within a glance of the blue marble again.

I missed it.

“Hey, Lieutenant.” Min Zhao had been up near the rock tunnel for a few seconds.

“What’s up, Max?”

She threw something in an easy curve through the air at me. I caught it and looked down. A small drive. “What is this?”

Zhao shrugged. “Smuggle mail. Been handed person to person all the way here. Came in with the new batch shipped up from home.”

“Anyone have a screen?”

Vorhis lifted his mattress up. “I’m not supposed to have this,” he muttered.

“I know,” I said, and plugged the drive in.

I’d asked what this was. But I already had a good idea. My mother’s face appeared on the screen. “Hey, son,” she said. “Hopefully, this gets to you safely.”

I sat down on the ground and put a finger up to the screen.

“By now, you might know we took a chance during the Rochester camp riots to get away from our minders. We don’t blame you for what you did. What any son would have done.”

But my father was not in the video.

“The Accordance is saying they need fighters. They need our help. So, we’re demanding independence. Earth for humans. If they really need our help, now is the time for them to give us our freedom back. I know some might disagree, they might say they’re the lesser evil. But can we really lay down our lives just to end up back under the Accordance if we help them win their war?”

Even though it had just been months since we’d been split apart, she looked older. There was a scar on her chin, and she’d cut her hair short. Almost military short. She wore a simple vest with extra pockets.

Were they still protesting? Or had they gone deeper

underground? She was filming her message in a tent, I could see.

She looked thinner.

"Just remember this, Devlin. You've made a name for yourself. You did something amazing out there, on the other side of the moon. People listen to your words. They look up to you. Keep that in mind as you make your decisions. Because we're all going to be making some tough choices soon. For Earth. For everyone. Be safe, son."

I looked up from the blank screen and saw Ken regarding me. Alpha squad was back and shucking. Delta getting ready to walk on out to guard duty.

"They don't know," Ken said. "Yours or mine. They don't know."

"Yours love you and admire you being here," I said. "Not the same."

Ken walked over, still in full armor, as everyone pretended not to listen. "Yeah, they're all in now," he said with a bitter twist of his lip. "My sister died when an Earth First protestor set off a bomb in front of the Cairo Arvani embassy; my father still has a limp. Back then, he was a delegate, trying to broker calm, get what he could for many. After that, it was different. Anyway, they're not that thrilled I'm under the command of the son of known anti-Accordance terrorists."

"You still hold anger about it? Me?"

Ken grimaced. "I buried it for a while. Still hung on to it, maybe even as late as Titan. Now?"

"Now?"

"Don't have any anger to waste," Ken said. "I spent it all on other things. Anything I have left, I'm saving up for Zeus."

"Captain Calamari," I said. Our nickname for the Arvani commander when he'd been in charge of us back on Icarus Base.

"Yes," Ken said reflectively.

"I doubt we'll ever see sucker-face again," I said.

"Everyone should have something they hope for," Ken said. "Little things that give us a reason to wake up."

Another shift. Another change. Another day guarding doors. This time not Pcholem but munitions stores. And the corridors were empty. People being moved to carriers.

But not us.

Whatever was going to happen, forward or retreat, was going to happen without the Rockhoppers.

Amira pulled me aside, her eyes flashing slightly from the nano ink buried deep inside her irises. "Bad news," she said quietly.

"I don't want to hear it," I told her. "Let's just stand here and wait for whatever's coming."

"There's ghost sign in the network," she whispered. "Just like back on Titan. I can sense little things. We're compromised. Hacked. Something. It came aboard with all the new arrivals."

"What the fuck do you want to do about it?" I asked her, tired. "We're not on patrol. We're just supposed to stand here. Report what you've found and let it go up channel."

"*They're* here," Amira hissed. "They're here and that's what matters. Not how the Accordance deals with it. But how we survive it. You and I both know how the ghosts can get inside a place like this."

Because they looked just like us, I thought.

Or maybe the ghosts *were* us. The one we'd captured looked like a human. Moved like a human. I'd risked my life to bring the body back, and the Accordance told us we'd be killed if we spilled the secret.

Or maybe the Conglomeration was already changing humans and using them against us.

The dead ghost on the moon hadn't told us anything. The Accordance hadn't told us anything.

We were fighting blind in the middle of a war between two giant civilizations.

"Nobody stays more than a few steps away from armor," I said. "You keep sniffing around. That's all we can do."

"We should be ripping this place apart." Amira folded her arms. "Why do you think we're standing around guarding munitions here?"

"Because even here, Arvani are outnumbered by humans. And the thousands of miners who have Earth First leanings are watching, waiting, and angry," I said. "But we stumble, and Zeus's family rips us apart. The Accordance does execute traitors. If our usefulness ends . . ."

"Finding ghosts is useful," Amira said.

"We sleep near our armor and I make sure we all look the other way when you slip out to go sniffing around," I told her.

Old habits. Old roles. She should be used to them by now.

"Listen, more and more people are being pulled into the asteroids. It's getting crowded. General infantry without armor. Engineers. Technicians. Miners."

"So we stay near armor, we stay near the weapons."

"We need more, Devlin. More information. More Accordance technology. More. Because when they eventually fall all the way back to Earth and then abandon it, we can't roll over."

"Do you think Shriek's people are still fighting back on his homeworld?" I asked. "Because I sure as hell don't."

"We can't just roll over," Amira repeated, and then shut up as Zizi Dimka came around the edge in armor.

"Something you should know," she said to me.

“What’s up?”

“We’re to all report back to the cave to the new platoon commander,” she said.

“New?”

“Squiddie,” Zizi said. “Just showed up. I walked over because it’s on the command channel and I can listen in on public. Figured you’d want a heads-up on this.”

“CPF is human,” I said.

“It said something about a riot and emergency powers,” Zizi said. “It’s agitated. All of us are to get down to the cave.”

“Fucking Arvani.” I looked around. “Okay, I guess we’re leaving the munitions doors unguarded, then.” The several feet of thick metal would have to hold shut without us.

15

The Arvani officer waited for us impatiently back at the entrance to our quarters. It wore standard encounter gear for outside the water: sculpted, form-fitting exoskeleton filled with water to keep it alive. Each of its eight arms was surrounded by jointed, powered segments.

But not armor. The exoskeleton was painted gaudy purple, red, and black, with red officer's marks near the Arvani's neck. These were the equivalent of fancy dress uniform for the Arvani when they were out of their pools of water and wandering about.

"You are delaying us!" it snapped. "Shape up, apes, we are required now!"

We all glanced at each other, and then the platoon looked at me and waited for orders.

The Arvani noticed this. His pupils narrowed and a single tentacle pointed at me. "You."

"What authority do you have to order this?" I asked. "The Colonial Protection Force is an independent volunteer organization. You have no command here. Who are you?"

It blew surprised bubbles in its helmet, where the vast bulk of its body resided. A few strange hues flashed across its skin. "I am Commander Sthenos," it bellowed via translation. Another motorized tentacle pulled out a pistol. "Articles of emergency have been declared throughout the interior of this habitat. You will arm up, and you will follow me."

Sthenos stalked across the rock toward the tunnel ways.

"Amira? Riot?" I asked.

"Three habitat levels of chaos," she said, eyes crinkling as she dove into the data. I waved a hand after the alien and nodded at the rest of the platoon. Follow the alien.

"We're not peacekeepers," I said, starting to walk after the Arvani commander. "We're soldiers."

"You are here. You are what we have in this location."

"Where are the carapoids? Struthiforms? Other Arvani?" I fell into pace beside Sthenos.

"They are elsewhere," Sthenos said irritably.

"Where?" I asked. "What's going on?"

"You are not cleared yet," Sthenos said. And I suspected that Sthenos, in his fancy Arvani gear and lack of armor, was probably not in the loop. This was a jumped-up supply clerk with a pistol, or some Arvani given a big title and shoved somewhere they thought wouldn't cause much trouble.

Sthenos didn't know what was going on any more than we did.

None of us had helmeted up yet. "I don't know much about riot control," Amira muttered. "But having been on the other side, I'm going to say that if we jump in with full armor and weapons hot, it's not going to cool things down any."

Shriek moved up to join us. The struthiform was in full armor, something he almost never did when inside an

Accordance structure. "I can hear it," he said. "It does not sound joyous."

"That it does not," I agreed. "Don't shoot; keep close to me. Amira, Ken, keep it low, but pass that around."

Sthenos forged on ahead, his metal-clad legs tapping on the rock as he scuttled along.

"Here we go," Amira warned. "Stay calm."

We burst out into a common cavern, mess halls on either side and the upper floors filled with dormitories accessed by metal walkways. Three thousand filled the common area. The small temporary gardens in the middle were already mud, trampled by angry feet in a packed scrum fighting against a handful of carapoids trying to hold the line.

A few open fires burned in the back, on the other side of the cavern. I helmeted up and peeked through it using the helmet's various displays and filters, but it wasn't being used to hide anything. They were just burning stuff ripped off the walls.

The crowd hissed like water tossed on a hot pan as we moved in.

"Be careful. We're suited up, they're not," I said.

"So, what the fuck are we supposed to do?" That was Zizi on the common channel.

I was still thinking. Looking at the massive press of bodies shoving the carapoids back up toward the wall.

Sthenos strode forward authoritatively and raised his pistol into the air.

"Oh, shit." I stepped forward as the crowd flinched, quieted, and started to stare at us.

"Cease this destructive behavior and return to your designated quarters," the Arvani officer shouted via amplification. The words rolled around the rocky roof, bouncing and echoing off the surfaces.

“We want to be evacuated too,” a short woman in a gray mining uniform shouted. She had a pipe in her hands.

“What are you talking about?” I started to ask, but Sthenos interrupted me with another loud command.

“Disperse or face consequences,” Sthenos shouted.

“Don’t say that,” Amira groaned on the public.

Sthenos snapped back, looking at the platoon.

I moved up past him and lowered my helmet to let the crowd see my face. I was a human being, not Arvani. The armor made us look like faceless machines, doubly so with helmet up. I wanted the crowd to see other human beings. I could hear other helmets snapping open around me as the platoon followed my lead.

Holding both hands up, palms out, I called out, “What evacuation?”

“The Arvani are all leaving. They’ve been boarding ships,” the miner with the pipe said. She stepped forward, suddenly realizing she was the closest thing to the group’s voice. The talking had created a momentary calm in the confrontation. I could see the carapoids edging over to us. I couldn’t tell anything from their expressions—the insect-like mandibles and eyes didn’t lead to much that I could recognize—and they didn’t say anything. “Everyone is running. They’re going to leave us here like they did on Titan. We want on the ships too.”

“There is no exodus,” Sthenos shouted. “You will stay at your posts and do your jobs. The fate of—”

“Fuck you, squiddie!” A bottle arced over the heads of the crowd nearest to us and struck Sthenos. The glass shattered and something oily splattered over the Arvani’s encounter suit.

The Molotov cocktail’s fire had guttered out as it had been thrown, luckily.

"Get behind us," I ordered the Arvani. "You're not helping matters."

But Sthenos spluttered and marched at the crowd. It raised its pistol. "I am *Arvani*, and I saw where that came from," it shouted. "There will be a consequence—"

"Fucking drag him behind us and get that gun out of his hands," I ordered, making a quick decision. We were in armor, but Sthenos would literally get pulled apart by the crowd if he started shooting into it.

Zizi and Aran from Alpha jumped the alien, disarming him and pulling back into the close wall of armor we'd made when forming up against the crowd.

That was a popular move. Cheers and hoots echoed around the cavern, and some laughter.

"This is insubordination," Sthenos screamed at us.

I moved another step forward and addressed the miner who'd been speaking, but loudly enough that everyone near the front of the crowd could hear us. "I don't know what is going on, but we haven't gotten the word to evacuate."

"That doesn't mean it isn't happening," she said.

"That's true," I admitted. "The Arvani are up to something, and they're not sharing. With any of us. Not even their junior officers." I pointed back at Sthenos, who was raging at Amira to try and get his pistol back.

"I don't want to get fucked," she said. "Everyone on Titan got left. People are saying we should talk to the Conglomeration now, broker some kind of deal for when they come. We're tired of being in the dark. We're not their tools."

"I understand," I said. "I know why you're doing it. You have to make your decision. But just know you are right. The Arvani don't care about your lives. Which means that when they come next, it will be like that Arvani back there. They'll start killing us. And in here, there's nowhere to run if they decide pacification is needed."

"Desperate times," she said.

"They are," I said. "But I think if we can keep together, organized, and use all the tools around us, we'll see Earth again. I truly believe that. Now, I'm going to back out through the corridor. You seem like you have some sway around here. See if you can keep them from bringing down something worse?"

"This is the only way they'll pay attention to us," she said. "We roll over, we go back to being in the dark."

"You do what you have to," I said. "But let me say this. The Pcholem, the ship attached to this asteroid, I've talked to it. And I have the impression it can expand and carry a lot. Until it leaves, your ride is going to be with the giant alien starship. Don't spook it. But if you're truly scared, send someone to talk to it. Or camp out near it . . . peacefully and calmly."

She nodded. "Okay."

"We're going to step back now," I said. "And take the carapoids with us. Is that good?"

Some shook their heads, but she nodded.

We backed out down the corridor and then let out held breaths of air as the bulkhead doors shut. One of the carapoids split off and approached us. Strong, spiked, and bony hands waved a pattern in the air. "Gratitude," it said simply. Then the massive beetle-like aliens trumped off down a fork and left us.

"I was hoping for a hug," Zizi said. "But that'll do."

"Give our Arvani officer his pistol back," I said. "Sir, we're sorry, but we had to talk them down."

Sthenos snatched his weapon back and pivoted around to look at all of us. "There will be consequences for your insubordination."

Consequences. Sthenos seemed to like that word a lot.

"I understand," I said. "I will take on responsibility for any reprimands that come as a result of the platoon following my direct orders."

Shriek moved. "The angry human mob has a point," he said. "All this dramatic behavior and running around while we wait for your homeworld to be destroyed is dreadful. Maybe you should broadcast surrender now. I'm sure the Conglomeration are wonderful and snuggly, like a mother on her eggs."

"Now's not the time for your jokes," I said.

"That. Is. Traitorous." Sthenos had frozen in place, staring at Shriek.

Amira groaned as Sthenos stalked toward the struthiform. "No humor," she said.

But Shriek seemed to know what he had done. He turned and faced the Arvani, wing hands folded by his body and his head cocked. "What do you think, Arvani? You didn't exactly help my homeworld, did you? Ran pretty fast once you all realized it was risky. Dragged us along to all your other fights. And here we still are."

"According to the common law of the Accordance unified military agreement," Sthenos said, rattling off the specific law that let him execute someone during a mutiny, "I condemn you to death as an enemy to the Accordance."

Shriek dropped his helmet and stepped forward, large eyes on the Arvani energy pistol. "Do it, seafood," he hissed.

This wasn't happening. I knew Shriek wasn't a fan of the Arvani, but the naked anger usually showed up in other forms. Not suicide by Arvani officer.

Sthenos's tentacle tip moved its grip on the pistol to fire. Amira knocked it clear, the pistol bouncing down the rock corridor. "Treason!" The Arvani spun around and looked at us all. "Detain her and hand me your weapon!"

"No," I said, "We're not going to do that. We need our medic." There was a thud in the distance. I wasn't sure what it was.

"You face the gravest repercussions." Sthenos looked at us all, realizing there was no help to be found, and then bolted for his gun.

"Quick," I shouted, and Ken was already by my side. Amira got there first, though, rocketing off a wall to strike the Arvani in the center of his upper tank. Metal cracked and creaked as she struggled to hold onto him in the middle of the eight flail ing tentacles that beat against her armor. She was punching and grabbing at something inside the Arvani encounter suit, ripping it out. The comms. She was silencing his ability to call out. I hadn't even thought about that.

I grabbed tentacles whipping about. "Stop struggling, we just want to talk." In the background, again, another thud. Loud enough that I glanced around, trying to figure out what it was.

There was a keening, bubbling sound. I realized that was an Arvani scream, raw and untranslated. Completely freaking out. Hell, so was I. We'd laid hands on an Arvani officer.

"Rope," Amira said calmly. "Now!"

She was jamming her thumbs into joints in the Arvani's powered legs, crushing the metal until something inside snapped and the limbs stopped moving. Then she bashed in the speakers that let the Arvani speak with her elbow.

Someone passed up some kind of paracord and a roll of utility tape. The alien stuff that was vacuum-rated. Amira and I wrapped the Arvanai's limbs together and then sat down with it between us. I looked at her, the question plain on my face.

"We need to crack him out of this suit and shove him out the shit-lock," she said, referring to our crude bathroom against the asteroid's hull.

"It's a long way from here to there. And . . ." We weren't executing Arvani officers.

"Asshole officers go overboard," Amira said. "Old naval ships. Happened all the time."

"This isn't the age of sail," I hissed.

"It might not be, but we're going to hang if we don't get rid of this."

"Why did you do this?" Shriek asked.

"He was going to shoot you," I said.

"So? This was not your fight." Shriek flicked a wing hand. "And what are the chances that even an Arvani would execute a vested officer of the Accordance?"

"I don't know," I shouted at him. "That's just it! It certainly looked about to shoot to me."

"Even if it did, it would only have cost that Arvani everything and meant no attention would be paid your insubordination." Shriek whistled impatiently. "My life is mine to do with what I please. I have been dead since the moment I watched my homeworld burn. I accepted this long ago. I make choices about how to live, how long to live, and when. *Not you.* Now you are all doomed. This is an utter waste. I am filled with despair that I have known your names."

There was another thud. I looked up as dust filtered through the air, shaken loose by the asteroid shaking. "That's the third time; what is that?"

Then the atmosphere-loss alarms kicked on, the annoying whine piercing my skull and near dizzying me.

Helmets snicked up and I got on the public channel. "What the hell was that?"

As if to answer me, an all-call went out, loud and crisp on the public channel. "Hull breach. Full vacuum protocol in effect. Everyone is to be in suits or near aid stations at all times. All CPF are to report up the chain of their command immediately."

"Pressure loss or attack?" I asked Amira.

"They'd call it out if it were battle stations."

"Not on the public. Not with people rioting because they're scared they're about to get left behind like everyone did on Titan." I looked around and then back down at our captured Arvani officer.

"Good point," Amira said. "Let me hop my way up . . . oh, here we go."

"Hello, Third Platoon. This is Colonel Vincent Anais again. I can't reach your temporary Arvani commander, so I'm pinging your command channel."

"Yes sir," I said, and then tried to talk right past his implicit query about the alien tied up by our feet. "What's going on?"

"Congratulations, you stuck around long enough to get off crap detail and for me to need you. There's a full-blown mutiny."

"We just dealt with the rioters," I said. "We calmed them down." Sthenos wriggled about, halfheartedly trying to get out from under our knees where we'd pinned him to the rocky asteroid floor.

Tony Chin was swearing to himself in Mandarin, I realized. What were we doing? "Chin, shut it down," I hissed.

"Not where you are," Anais said, almost over me. "We've had human crews working with Arvani specialists around the clock to finish the Trojan conversions. Very hush-hush, but they've been turning the Trojans into carriers. Low-budget, retrofitted carriers. This is to get the numbers we need back to Titan. To retake what we've lost. But—"

Another thud. We instinctively crouched for a second.

Anais swore. That was new. There was a moment of quiet, and then he came back on. "So, the human crews working on two of the Trojans mutinied. They're ostensibly under an Earth First banner. They've demanded the release of Rina Joseph, Alois Kincaide, and Alan Coatzee from Accordance jails."

I recognized two of those names. Rina and Alois. People who'd once planned protests by my parents' side. I knew them as friendly smiles and laps I'd sat in. I hadn't realized they were jailed. Rotting away under the Accordance.

Anais continued. "But I think they're just panicked. Rumors of impending Conglomeration attacks are everywhere, and they saw what happened on Titan. Which is why we need these ships to get back to Titan, damn it."

"What're the loud noises?" Amira asked.

"We've been exchanging fire. Trying to knock out the weapons they have trained on us. Devlin, we've been keeping what we're doing here secret so that the Conglomeration doesn't know our next play. But now, if they see us shooting at each other here in trailing orbit, they're going to come out before we're ready for them. And it's going to be a big fucking mess. So you're going in. Welcome back to active."

"Why us?" I asked reflexively.

"I need someone who can think quick, think creatively, and not make a bigger mess."

"You're asking us to attack human beings who were building the ships we needed," Ken noted.

"You're attacking them only if they fight back or you can't figure out a way to resolve the situation," Anais replied. "And even if you have to make the worst choice, it could still well save everyone we love back on Earth. I'm not saying the job ahead of you is easy. But we're not here for easy choices; we're here to fight a war."

"What am I authorized to offer them, if they surrender?" I asked.

"*I'm told* we're past that point. I'm told that anyone you take alive, we will keep humanely jailed. Now get to airlock five-B; they're waiting for you. Handle this. Get back in the game."

And then he was gone.

I looked over at Ken and Amira. "We should go. It gives us options."

"Like what? Joining mutineers?" Ken hissed.

"Our choices are to flush the Arvani out a lock and pretend it didn't happen, or get to some kind of transport not controlled by Arvani," Amira said. "He's right, Ken. What do *you* want to do here?"

Ken half crouched in his armor. His face, behind his helmet, was obscured by reflections. I couldn't figure out what he was thinking.

"We can't kill the commander," he said. "Whatever we do, we cannot have the Arvani turn against the CPF. We do this, we destroy the freedom the CPF has gained for itself. We put more than our own lives at risk."

"Options are good," Amira said. "Let's tie our pet squiddie to a chair and get the hell out of here."

Within minutes, Sthenos was lashed tightly to one of the bunks back in our quarters. I turned away from Sthenos to face the platoon and explain the orders we'd just been given. "I won't force any of you to come with us, or force anyone to stay," I said to the entire platoon as they all arranged themselves around me, ready to head out with their full weapons kit and everything else they could think to carry packed and strapped. "You all have the choice."

I had more of a speech planned, but they all knew what was what.

"If we stay, Arvani will string us up to blame," Aran Patel said. "In Chennai, I saw them put an entire sector's police force to death for something a captain did. You made the call, we have to follow. One way or another. There's no real choice. We're expendable to them. You know that."

"Jesus, Patel, you make it sound like he personally sentenced you to death," Erica Li said with a snort.

"Well," Aran said calmly.

He wasn't wrong, I knew.

I was going to apologize, but Ken interrupted. "We've always been facing death when we're given commands. That is the nature of what we do. That is the nature of an order, a decision, when in war. Our choices become how we want to face death."

"Well, I'm not giving up my power armor," Aran said.

"Does anyone wish to stay?" Ken asked.

No one did.

"Then it's airlock five-B. The Arvani might be bastards, but if the Conglomeration figures out we're in the middle of a mutiny, everyone else around here is going to be dead. Let's move!" Ken shouted.

17

We were shot out of airlock five-B in all-too-familiar reentry capsules, little more than a heat shield with some thrusters and a parachute we didn't need. Inside the claustrophobic coffin, my helmet an inch from the heat shield, I tried to relax as we tumbled through the half-mile gap of empty space.

No thrusters to adjust course; that would reveal us. We drifted slowly, like seeds thrown onto the wind.

"First barrage," Anais informed us. "To keep them busy."

We heard nothing. We couldn't, in the cold vacuum. Hundreds of beams of light would be stabbing at the other ships, and missiles would be lobbed. And I waited in the dark of the windowless capsule.

"Chaffing out," Anais said.

We would come with a wave of confusing, glittering dust, bouncing signals every which way around us.

"Okay," Amira said. "What's the plan? We join up with Earth First? Or we take the carrier ship for ourselves?"

"Can *you* fly a carrier ship?" I asked Amira. "Because it

seems like a large number of technicians and specialists are on it right now. The large crews are for a reason?"

"We don't even know if *they* can fly it," Amira said. "All we know is that they took one over."

"But you can't fly one."

Amira was silent for a moment. I imagined her grinding her teeth. "No."

"Then we're going to need to ally ourselves with them. Or . . ."

"Or what?" Ken asked.

"Or we help quell the mutiny and face what comes next," I said. "Because those ships are to retake Titan. To protect Earth. With human crews. There is a war. And what are we going to do? Join the Conglomeration?"

"I will die first," Shriek said.

"We know what they do to planets," Tony Chin said. The three sergeants didn't normally interrupt the squad command channel, but he sounded very sure of his opinion. "I'm not doing that."

"I was just thinking out loud."

"Devlin, pick a course and follow it," Ken snapped. "Lead. You are our leader. This is your job. Embrace it and stop trying to hand it away."

"I'm not going to kill any humans who are putting their lives at risk to do what's right," Amira said. "Putting this mutiny down? I'd rather join it and flip the damn Accordance my middle finger."

"Amira—" The thrusters lit up, shoving me face-first against the inner side of my capsule. Then it peeled itself away from me and I hung in the air for a second, coasting toward a large pitted landscape of rock.

Shriek jumped back in on the common channel. "I will

turn myself over after this. I will claim I did it all. The Arvani—"

"Shriek, shut up," I ordered. "We deal with this first. Then we'll sort that out. Everyone, get your head in *this* game, right here and right now."

"We're here," Ken grunted.

The capsules left us with enough momentum that we gently struck the rock in a rain of tiny silver chaff. Laser light flickered in the air around us, madly trying to carve up the remains of our capsules that still hung above the hull.

"Hopefully, the Accordance won't start shooting too," I said.

We stuck to the hull. Somewhere inside the ship were Accordance gravity plates. I'd felt the faint flip inside my stomach that was the pull of gravity as we'd approached.

It wasn't very strong out here. Moon level, maybe. It would increase as we moved down and in toward the core.

"Contact," Zizi shouted on the common channel. "I found an airlock."

"Devlin, what are we doing?" Lana Smalley asked.

I looked at the twinkling chaos between the Trojans and the crude, rocky carrier we were hanging on to. A split second of thought. "Try not to kill them," I said. "But we're going to put this down and take the carrier."

"For the Accordance?" Amira asked suspiciously. "Or for ourselves?"

"I don't fucking know yet," I said. "But either way, try to keep them alive if you can keep yourselves out of risk."

Then I let go of the side and kicked my way down toward Zizi.

A long arc of light danced across the pits and craters of the rocky hull, lighting everything up with harsh white and casting long shadows. "What the hell was that?"

"They've got hull welders," Zizi said, almost bemused.

"They don't want to let us in through the airlock, apparently."

With a loud bang, I spun around and bounced off rock. I steadied myself. "They're shooting. With what?"

"They've got some kind of jury-rigged rail gun. Three o'clock," Min Zhao said. "Everyone, take cover."

"Don't return fire!" I shouted.

18

I scrabbled my way forward to join someone sheltering behind a dip in the hull. It was Chandra Khan.

"You okay, Chaka?" I asked.

"It's going to be hard to get into that airlock without hurting someone," Khan said.

Amira popped onto the command channel again. "I have another interesting question I think we need to mull."

"Right now?" A piece of metal slammed into the rock hull, sending shards flying everywhere. I winced as the debris rattled against my armor.

"Now's as good a time as any to get our heads straight," Amira said. "We need to know what's happening. What we're doing. And you need to make some calls. Because you're the leader here."

"Okay, what's wrong?" I wanted to rub my forehead.

"Ghost sign," Amira said. "I have to keep my head down; I can't help in the usual ways or it'll spot me. It's strong."

"So the Conglomeration is here," Ken said.

"How is that even possible?" Min Zhao demanded. "They

were buried under the ground on Titan. But how are they on a carrier ship, here in the Trojans? How are they fucking popping up everywhere?"

"Don't worry about how," Ken said, his voice reassuring and calm. "Just worry about the fact that this mutiny is not what it seems."

Things were shifting around again. Our plan to maybe sneak off somehow was fading. If there were Conglomeration here, ghosts here, something else was going on.

"This answers a question I have," Ken said.

"Which is?" I asked.

"Where are the other platoons on this attack?"

I glanced up in the sparkling debris between us and the Trojan docks. No more shooting. No more drama.

"We're it. There were other CPF around that might even have been closer," Amira agreed. "Why us?"

"You think they're suiciding us?" Lana Smalley asked. "Or using us as a diversion? Maybe they already know about Sthenos."

I was lying with my back against the rock hull, still staring out into space. I could hear the tension in my sergeants' voices. Smalley, Chin, and Zhao hadn't attacked their Arvani commander. They'd been taking my orders calmly for long enough. They'd put themselves at risk for so long.

"They sent just us because of the ghost sign," I said on the platoon's common channel, taking the debate out of command loops. "Anais, his techs, they must have spotted it. So they sent us."

"I don't understand," Smalley said.

"When Amira sniffed out the ghost sign back on Titan, it was because she was familiar with the patterns and code," I said.

"Devlin. What are you doing?" Ken sounded nervous. That was a first.

"Time to let the Rockhoppers in on the great big fucking secret," I said. "We captured a ghost. Back at Icarus Crater."

"What?" I wasn't even sure who shouted that in shock. "We're supposed to get clear of them. How?"

"Luck," I said. "But we know what we're fighting. Accordance claims we need to pull back and let heavy forces in. But what they want is to not let humans find out what the ghosts are."

"They're human," Amira said.

"What the fuck are you talking about?" Smalley asked. "What do you mean, human?"

"They look like us. Inside this carrier, it could be anyone. They look like us. Ghosts look like us," Ken said.

"Why haven't you told us these things before?" Smalley continued.

"We were under very strict orders," I said.

"Bullshit! Either we're all in this together, or the three of you are just as useless as the squiddies," Smalley snapped.

"Could they be sending us out here to die with that information?" someone asked.

"I don't know," I said. "But you all need to know what we're facing in there."

There was cursing in four different languages on the common.

"But what does it mean?" Ilyushin asked, frustrated.

"It means they need us," Ken said.

Everyone quieted. "Go on," I said.

"I've been thinking about this since Titan," Ken explained. "The Conglomeration are using humans. Or something that looks human. The Accordance, they're putting us into carrier ships like this one. They're using us to build more ships. They wouldn't be doing all of this, either of them, if they didn't *need* us. The only reason humans took these ships over is because they were *building* them. The Arvani, they just don't have the numbers. There are only a handful of Pcholem in the system. Even the struthiforms are dying off because they lost their homeworld, their nesting grounds."

"How the fuck does that help us right here, right now?" Vorhis asked.

"Because we've assumed, since the day the Accordance came to orbit and pacified Earth, that it was about them. Their tools. Their abilities. Their technology. But the truth is, they're fighting over us right now. That's their weakness."

"How the hell is them ripping us apart to fight over us a weakness?" The common channel devolved into angry voices.

"No," I shouted. "Ken's right."

The common channel settled down.

"Anais sent us in because we know what ghosts are," I said. "We're not joining the Conglomeration. We're not going to slaughter these people either, which is what the Arvani would want. They have skills we're going to need soon."

"When?" Ilyushin asked.

"When humanity gets out from under them all," I said.

"That sounds like Earth First talk," Ilyushin noted.

"Well, I *am* the son of famous Earth First terrorists," I said. "What the hell were they expecting?"

I used my fingertips to skim along the hull.

"Where are you going?" Amira asked.

"To disable anyone firing at us with a homemade rail gun. Then we're going to break in and, bulkhead by bulkhead, carefully retake this place without killing them. We're wearing alien-designed power armor, built to take full combat hits. This is a one-sided battle."

I flung myself over the rocky lip and toward the two spacesuits by the airlock.

"They might get lucky," Amira shouted as slugs slammed into my helmet. For brief seconds, liquid metal streamed down the side of my vision as they obliterated themselves against the shielding.

"True," I said. "So I'll have to move quickly."

And before I'd even finished muttering that, I was between the mutineers. They struggled to draw on me, but I snatched the weapons away, crushed them between my armored fingers, and shook my head.

19

Patel came running down the corridor. "Fire in—"

The explosion came right behind him before he'd finished his warning. The flames enveloped him, throwing him forward and into a nearby bulkhead.

Alpha squad shot forward, Zhao taking point.

"Patel?" I called out.

"Fine," he said. "I'm fine."

"Go back and join Taylor, have Shriek look you over."

"I'm *fine*," Patel gritted.

"Do it anyway."

Patel stood up and moved to the back with our twenty captives. Engineers, miners, maintenance workers, all zip-tied together and looking somewhat dazed. Lilly Taylor sat with them. One of the rail guns had punched through her shin guard. Shriek had filled the hole in her with a gel and pumped some painkillers in, and she was ready to get back into the mix. But I had her guarding the captives.

"Hart?" Zhao called out on the command channel.

"Yes?"

“We have a situation.”

I looked down through the clearing smoke. “Yeah?”

We’d cut our way down into the carrier. Delta had our asses covered, and Alpha and Bravo were taking turns blowing up doors and pushing forward. We were rolling up resistance and zip-tying them to each other as we went.

It was slow and tedious corridor work. We’d been at it for an hour.

I kept to the side of the corridor and moved up to the front, crouching down by Erica Li, who was covering with her rifle the next bit we’d have to leapfrog into. She pointed down the corridor. Bulkhead doors were open down the corridor. A straight run.

Too good to be true. We’d been fighting through thick steel door after thick steel door. Designed to frustrate invaders like us and keep the carrier airtight no matter the scenario.

The mutineers had kept them all shut to slow us down.

Now they were throwing out the welcome mat?

Someone slowly put their hands out from behind a bulkhead into the open space. “We want to talk,” a voice shouted into the open space between us.

Zhao was lying against the bulkhead, looking straight at me. “Second verbal request,” she said.

I closed my eyes and thought the command to slide my helmet back down. My nostrils burned. The acrid smoke from the explosives still in the air seared the back of my throat. Not my brightest move; I could have used the amplification in the suit.

But responding in kind felt like the right move. “Hello,” I shouted. “What would you like to talk about?”

“We’re willing to talk, but only to someone we choose that you’ll have to bring over.”

“Okay,” I agreed. “Who is it that we have to bring over?”

Zhao lowered her helmet and crabbed over to me. “There’s some equipment I’m seeing farther down the corridor,” she whispered. “I think it’s an even bigger rail gun they’ve wheeled into place.”

“Fucking engineers,” I hissed. And then louder. “Who are we bringing over?”

“Devlin Hart,” the voice shouted back.

I laughed. I couldn’t help it. I looked at Zhao, who shrugged, the action taken up by the heavy armored shoulders.

“Bring us Devlin Hart,” the voice shouted. “No armor. Hart can negotiate with us. If anyone in armor steps up, we start shooting.”

“You’re a popular guy,” Amira said.

I stood up.

“What are you doing?” Zhao stiffened.

“Shucking,” I said. My armor, at a mental command, began to crack itself open. I stepped forward and out, feeling totally naked in just my gray basic wear.

“Rockhoppers don’t shuck,” Zhao said.

“They want to talk. I’m going in. Ken, hold the corridor. If I’m not back in an hour, you get to make the big decisions.” He came up beside me and I grabbed his armored shoulders, feeling small beside him. “You’ll get your platoon, Ken.”

His helmet slid away and Ken’s dark eyes blinked. “I will not be doing that,” he said. “If they capture you, I’ll be in to take you back out. You are the commander here.”

There was something more I wanted to say, but Amira stalked up next to me and stopped. Her armor began to lean back and peel itself off her.

“They didn’t ask for Amira Singh,” I told her.

“It’s buy-one-get-one-free day for Rockhoppers,” she said.

"You're not going in alone. Ghost sign is increasing, I want to get in closer and sniff. I'm not going to sit here while decisions about our future get made down there."

Ghost sign. Right. This wasn't just mutineers we were dealing with. The Conglomeration had its fingerprints on all this.

I stepped out with my hands up. "It's your lucky day," I called out. "Because I'm actually Devlin Hart."

"Bullshit," the voice down the corridor said.

"It's me, I swear," I said. "I'm coming forward with Amira Singh."

A face peeked quickly around the bulkhead. I recognized it. "Mr. Dismont. From Shangri-La Base."

Dismont stepped out into the open as well. "Holy shit, it's really you."

I stepped hesitantly forward. "I'm just going to keep walking forward with my hands where you can see them, Amira as well, and we'll talk."

20

I faced the council of mutineers in a room deep inside the carrier's shielded core after being silently trooped past corridors lined with construction workers holding crude, cobbled-together weapons. Arc welders, unwieldy rail guns, and other contraptions I wasn't sure about.

This was the heart of the insurrection: ten tired engineers, gangly men and women with screens strapped to their forearms, staring at us without saying a thing.

"Why did you call for me?" I finally asked.

"When everyone ran on Titan, you stayed behind," Dismont said. "Many of those engineers were tasked to work here on these carriers. We know who you are. We trust you. We will talk to you. We want you to get us a cease-fire to get us some time."

"What do you think you can do? Run to the Conglomeration?" I asked.

"No," Dismont shook his head, exasperated. "It was never that. Conglomerate messages are all over the networks, I know that. Offers to leave us alone if we defect. Preserve a place for us as we are. Promises of power and technology. Promises of land. We don't buy it."

"Then what the hell is all this?" I asked.

"It began with protest," he told us both. "Understand, since we got here from Titan, they've thrown us into this project full bore. We work long days, and we work dangerous situations. The workers on the carriers are suffering from blowouts, and they're expected to work without suits, as the gloves slow them down. We complained, but nothing changed. Everything was rush-rush. Good men started dying. One, airlock accident; one, a tunnel boring blowout. They kept stacking up. We kept holding services.

"Five hours ago, there was a memorial service for three tunnel borers who died after a seal breach. The Arvani sent carapoids to break it up and get us back to work. We were angry. We broke and fought back, refusing to leave. Demanding better safety. More rest time so mistakes aren't made. We know we're in the middle of a war. It's one thing to risk your life for it. It's another to see our lives spent so cheaply."

That rang true. I glanced over at Amira. She wasn't paying attention. Her eyes were half closed. She was focused on ghost sign.

"So, what's the play?" I asked. "My team was just the first wave of what they can send at you. You going to make a stand here?"

"We're going to run," Dismount said. "We can *fly* this thing, Devlin. All we need is some time."

Amira cocked her head. Something was going on in that invisible world of hers. "And where will you run to?" I asked him.

"We have the entire solar system to hide in. Get away from all this. All we need is time so we can continue getting the engines up. We need you to get us time," Dismont pleaded.

I wanted to join him. Run for somewhere in the dark and hide from everything we'd seen. Everything we'd been asked to do. Forced to do.

"There's a problem with that plan," Amira said, opening her eyes.

Dismont frowned and looked at her. "What's that?"

"The engines aren't ever coming on."

Shit. I recognized Amira's ready stance. It would have looked casual if I hadn't seen it before. She had relaxed a bit, a friendliness in her face. But her feet had moved into a more stable position. Her neck was angled just ever so slightly forward. The faintest grin on the corners of her lips. But behind the silver eyes, there would be nothing but a spring being slowly compressed.

Here we go, I thought, and half turned toward the engineers with the hand-built weapons aimed at us.

Amira snapped forward and twisted behind a nearby engineer, shoving a carbon fiber knife from up between her fingers into the side of his neck. "No one fucking move," she said calmly, pulling him back toward the wall with her so that she could keep everyone in front of them.

"Fuck," I hissed, holding my hands up in the air and stepping between her and the guns.

Dismont was crushed and confused. "Whoa," he shouted, "everyone calm down, calm down. She hasn't hurt Chris."

Yes, I thought. Let's stay cool. "What are you doing with Chris?" I asked Amira.

"Chris is a Conglomeration spy," Amira said. "I've been tracking him. So, I repeat myself: Those engines won't come on. Only your weapons that are facing the Trojans will work. Everything else has been disabled. You're being used."

Dismont stepped hesitantly forward. "That's a hell of an accusation."

"It's what she does," I said. "She finds this stuff. She found them out on Titan. She found them out when they attacked Icarus Base."

I hated invoking Icarus. But the moment I did it, I could see the engineers paying close attention and looking at each other.

"On Icarus Base, Amira tracked the Conglomeration as they attacked. She kept us alive. And if you want to survive, you'd better damn well listen to her," I continued.

"I've worked with Chris inside the engines for a month," one of the mutineers said. "He saved my life down there."

"This is insane," Chris said from behind me. I wanted to turn around and look at Amira. I wanted to mouth the word "ghost?" I wanted to get a nod or a shake of the head so I knew what was standing just behind me.

Instead, I swallowed. "We can test this."

Dismont looked at Chris and Amira and then back to me. "How?"

"I get you your time. I call it in. Time enough for you to fire those engines and see if they work. Or if Amira's right. Time enough to test your weapons, too. Okay? If you can fire them, if everything is good, then we have a second conversation. That sound good?"

Tension hung heavy, but eventually Dismont nodded. Weapons weren't lowered, but they were relaxed.

I slowly turned back to Amira. "Do you want to—"

Chris yanked free of Amira, throwing her back up against the wall with a single shove of the hand. She left a bright ribbon of blood along his throat as she was tossed back and hit the wall with a loud thud. Amira leapt forward after him.

"Hey!" one of the engineers shouted as he stepped in front of Chris.

Chris punched him in the face. Blood sprayed into the air and the man dropped, skull shattered and face a sudden mess of flesh, blood, and brain. Then Chris sprinted through the door.

One of the shocked engineers had the presence of mind to shoot a rail gun a second too late. The bullet smacked the rim of the door.

"Ghost?" I asked.

"Yes. It's mine!" Amira snarled, picking up the knife knocked loose when she'd hit the wall. She exploded out the door.

Dismont was on his knees by the killed engineer. "Jesus," he said, in shock. He put a hand down on the ground, unsteady.

I squatted next to him, trying to ignore the bloody mess that had been a person's head. I put a hand on his shoulder. "Chris isn't what anyone thought. Chris is Conglomerate. A ghost." No sense in fighting to keep all that a secret. It was time to explain things. Because I had no idea how long any of us were going to live now.

"A ghost?" I had the attention of everyone.

"Yes. And it talked you into this mutiny, I'll bet. I'll bet Chris was all over the place, giving you all suggestions. Getting you to trust him. But now we need to figure out why this, why now?" I was betting it meant more shit was about to come down on us. Forget the Accordance wanting our asses. It was Conglomeration about to try and kill us now. "Get control of your ship. It won't be able to meddle with things now that Amira is openly hunting it. Get your scanners up. Open channels to CPF. Surrender. But get yourself facing outward. Get your weapons ready. See what I'm saying?"

Dismont looked at me, eyes wide with tears and rage. "Yes."

Good. Angry was good. "I'm going after Amira. Get my

platoon in here. Call them in. With armor." Rockhoppers didn't shuck.

"I will," I heard Dismont say as I ran out into the corridor.

Where had Amira gone? I ran full tilt until I saw blood. Spatters of it on the ground.

They'd engaged. There was an indentation in one of the walls. I kept running. Found a body, twisted unnaturally and tossed aside. For a second, my breath caught. Then I saw the coveralls. Not Chris. Not Amira. Some unfortunate person, her long hair wet with blood, who had just been in the way.

I dug deep and ran even faster. Then almost tripped over Amira at a corner as I skidded to a stop. She crouched against a wall, covered in blood. For a second, I thought she was crying. I moved slowly toward her.

"Amira?"

She looked at me, shivering. Chris's body was at her feet. Lifeless. His throat had been torn out, and Amira still held wet tissue in one hand.

"Amira?"

The second time, her name got her attention. She looked at me, blood smeared across her face. Shit. She *was* crying.

"You're okay," I said softly to her. "You're okay." I put a hand on her shoulder.

"I know I'm okay," she said. "I'm angry. I tried to capture it alive. I really, really fucking tried. We could have gotten it to talk. Figured it out. But I had to kill it. It got my knife away. It got the upper hand."

I looked down. "You did what you had to."

Amira looked down at her hand and opened it. Then wiped her hand against a thigh. "Fuck, Devlin. I was so close."

I looked at the body. The walls shivered and buckled

slightly; booms echoed through the corridor. "What's that?" I asked.

"Contact," Amira said with a sigh. "We're under attack."

"Who?"

"Everyone, apparently." Atmosphere-loss alarms triggered. Amira wiped the back of her hand against her cheek, smearing more blood around. She took a step forward and buckled.

I grabbed an arm and pulled it over my shoulder, and we ran together for safety.

21

Platoon members turned to look at us as we staggered in. They stared at Amira, and I shook my head. Catching the signal, almost everyone found something else to pay attention to. The engineers did not. Their jaws dropped, unable to take their eyes off the blood-splattered Amira.

Ken thudded over. "Your armor's in the corner," he said. Shriek, helmet down, paced back and forth near one of the walls, raggedy feathers puffed and his head bobbing oddly.

"Shriek, there are people in the corridors who're hurt. See if you can set up treatment, coordinate what you can," I said.

Shriek paused, cocked his head. "Okay," he said. "Thank you."

He took off.

Amira brushed past him and headed right for her armor. I watched her nestling down into the gaping maw of opened armor, and then saw Ken's expression. "What?"

"You've been offline for almost half an hour." He leaned closer. "In the meantime, three Conglomerate ships came in at speed on a high angle of attack. Most of the carriers and human-operated ships did not return fire. Sabotage. Mutinies. Everyone had to scramble to figure out what was happening."

"Situation now?" I beckoned him to follow me as I walked up to my armor.

"They were on an attack run. They've swept through, done the damage. Chatter says something on the order of four or five thousand CPF dead; they're tallying things up." Shit, I thought, as I turned around and backed into my armor. It made contact with the back of my neck, and the stinging sensation of neural synchronization passed as I closed my eyes and tried to pretend that alien technology wasn't wriggling its way into my spinal cord. "We think there might be a slower, secondary-stage attack on the way to take the Trojans. But defenses are getting spun up. Rumor is that some Accordance assets are heading in. But that isn't the big news we need to be worrying about right now."

My armor folded itself around me. I opened my eyes and looked at Ken. "What more do we need to worry about?"

"Anais is coming in. With two platoons. They're on the hull and getting ready to board."

"Is he coming for us?"

"I don't know," Ken said. "I left Delta to be a welcoming party for them. Whatever kind of welcome we need. All he's said to me was to wait for him to board."

"No mention of . . ." I looked around at the engineers making calls and coordinating repairs. The Conglomeration had gotten several good hits in. Amira had routed us around unsafe corridors to get us to the core. I lowered my voice. ". . . our little problem back on the Trojans?"

"No."

"Amira, can you help them with their ship?" That would get her focused on something besides the damn ghost she'd killed. Taking her along to meet Anais right now might not be the best move.

She nodded, a little distant. "Yes. I can do that."

"Thank you." I nodded at Ken. "Let's go see what we need to do about Anais."

"Okay." Once more out into the mess of it all, I thought as Ken's helmet snapped up.

Anais came through a service airlock with his platoons spreading out in front of him like a metallic shockwave. Once the bay was secure, the nervous engineers with their handmade weapons gently pushed back out into the corridors, I moved forward. A wall of crimson-painted armor parted to let me through.

"Hello, Hart," Anais said, helmet down, looking me over. "You have the ship. Well done."

"I'm not sure—" I started to say.

"Oh, you did well. The leadership of the carrier, who had been under the threat of a Conglomerate spy holding them hostage, contacted us once they were freed and worked to help get systems back online to try and help us fight the attack. Now we're all gearing up for the second wave that's on its way. Couldn't have done it without you, Hart. Well done, soldier."

We were face to face now.

Ken shook his head. "We were supposed to kill them all for you; now you're saying they were never really a mutiny? What the hell is this?"

Anais leaned forward. Then, slowly, he repeated himself. "The leadership of the carrier helped get systems back online to fight the Conglomeration after the hero of the Darkside

War killed a Conglomerate plot to take the carrier over. What do you not understand?"

"The fact that it is not true," Ken gritted.

"But it *is* true," Anais said. "And if you disagree, Ken, you put the lives of every single one of those engineers in here at risk. If they're truly mutineers of their own design, then they're to spend the rest of their lives in jail or face execution for treason against the Accordance. So, Ken, what happened here? Truly?"

"This is playing public relations; this isn't about the war." Ken folded his arms.

Anais leaned in close, grabbing Ken's neck ring. "War *is* public relations, son. It's about how to bring the coffins home. Triumphantly, or secretly. It's about telling everyone at home the enemy is so evil that unless we throw all our might against them, all is lost. It's about convincing ourselves we're all on the same page or it all falls apart. There is no war without PR. Never has been."

"So, you're saying the Conglomeration are not evil?" Ken shot back.

With a laugh, Anais let go of Ken. "Hell no, Awojobi. They're evil as all fuck. What I'm asking is, do you want all these engineers here so we can pilot some of these carriers back to Titan, along with the rest of the CPF, and take back Titan? Or do you want to stand here and debate CPF operational tactics?"

Ken's eyes widened. "We're going back?"

"If your folks will lower their defense screens, I have an entire company waiting to jump out into the dark and over to the hull. We boogie out, but we leave enough hardware back here to keep fighting the next wave of Conglomeration coming for the Trojans. I'm here to retake Shangri-La and rescue more of our people. See the big picture, Awojobi?"

"And we're coming with you?" I asked warily, waiting for some kind of trap to snap shut on us.

Anais turned his focus on me. "You hoping to stay behind, Hart? Or does all this sound too good to be true?"

"Seems like a very sudden reversal of fortune," I said carefully. "All things considered."

"Things like the very strange story that came out of your barracks?" Anais asked.

"What strange story would that be?" I projected nothing but puzzled curiosity. But inside, I felt like I was about to be tossed out of the bottom of a hopper dusting out on a fast drop.

"The unbelievable story of an Arvani officer who claims you disabled his suit and tied him to a bed frame, leaving him there during the attack."

I looked at Anais and cleared my throat. "That's—"

"Can you imagine that?" Anais interrupted. "The heroes of the Darkside War, who fought bitterly to the end on the plains of Shangri-La, the enders of the Trojan mutiny, tying an Arvani officer up like that? No one else could believe it either. His superiors felt a pack of mere humans couldn't be capable of that. It was a tall tale to justify an officer hiding away in a closet during an attack. And the struthiform officers were a bit unimpressed that this Arvani claimed to have been trying to execute a multiply decorated struthiform medic as a defense. Sthenos is no longer a problem."

"What happened?"

"Sthenos has been promoted," Anais said. "A delightful and cushy position that takes our mutual friend back to the moon. No active control of any fighting force ever again. And out of our hair."

"He gets promoted?" Ken hissed. "For incompetence?"

"Do anything like that to a remotely competent Arvani," Anais warned, a blank expression on his face, "you'll be executed within a day. And I'll be the one to explain why you all were traitorous bastards undeserving of the tag 'hero.' Understand, Arvani care about Arvani. So, you got off easy, and mainly because I'm absolutely pleased to find that the Rockhoppers' ability to do the right thing while still following orders is still in effect. That's not always an easy finesse."

"So glad to be there for you." The sarcasm dripped from Ken in the empty space.

Anais continued, ignoring it. "So, you get to go back with me. I'm to take Shangri-La, and I want you in my landing team so that when we broadcast the retaking of Shangri-La, the heroes of the Darkside War are the first on the ground for our cameras. The CPF needs the boost. I need the story. I haven't been putting my own ass on the line here with stunts like taking care of Sthenos because I like you. Got it?"

"We'll be there with you," I said.

"Fantastic," Anais said enthusiastically. "I'm going to give the good news to the rest of your platoon and start bringing everyone aboard. Let's get everyone here fired up to go take back what's ours!"

He headed out to the corridor, surrounded by armor.

"Everything that man says is a lie wrapped in truths to get you to do something he needs," Ken said, watching everyone file out.

"We have a chance to get back to Shangri-La and save people we had to leave behind." I shook my head. "That has to be worth it. We came out the other side of a real mess, Ken."

"We're pawns. All he wants is our triumphant return to the ground. Your celebrity. To get more people to join the CPF."

"They need recruits. We're in a war."

“Fucking Conglomeration,” Ken said wearily.

“It doesn’t matter how, or why, but we’re getting a chance to put a boot up their ass. Let’s take it.”

Ken nodded. “Yeah. Let’s go give Shriek the good news. We’re going back into the grinder. He’ll love a chance to tell us we’re all going to die.”

I snorted. “Our cheerful feathered friend owes us all drinks forever; I hope he realizes that.”

22

The platoon took over a small hold as the carrier began shaking itself up to speed. We were back to Rockhopper discipline: cleaning off our armor and checking it over. Taking stock of our weapons and sending different squad members off to the other teams to see what we could get from supplies, or beg and borrow from the other platoons that had come aboard.

No one strayed more than a few feet from their armor. Most of us rolled out blankets nearby, ready to jump up and in if needed.

"If CPF are dropping in, what are the others going to be doing?" Amira asked, forty-eight hours after we broke orbit. She had her EPC-1 in her lap and was stenciling bugkiller onto it with spray paint.

"Anais won't say," I told her.

"And that should tell us all something," Ken said.

"They are worried about leaks," Shriek said, lying down near the wall. "Can you blame them? This entire carrier now knows a secret the Arvani have been trying to keep from everyone since the start of the war. Something even I didn't know until Icarus Crater happened."

Amira looked up at one of the slightly warped bulkheads creaking as the carrier continued its acceleration. "There's a good chance this whole thing will fall apart before we even get to Titan. Problem solved."

"These are all desperation moves," Ken said in disgust. "Half-built ships taking hastily picked-up platoons, minimal supplies . . . Our first tactical move on the surface won't be anything that makes sense militarily; it'll be about securing ourselves a photo opportunity. Armed jumpships swooping in to drop off the heroes of the Darkside War. We're ordered to jump out with our helmets transparent. One sniper, one random cricket: we die. For *video*."

The platoon's squads were eavesdropping, I realized. Slowly cleaning weapons or playing cards, with bodies half turned toward us.

"This is a good thing," I said slowly. I'd been turning something over in my mind for a long time. Something Ken said. Something I kept coming back around to.

"Why do you say that?" Amira asked, eyebrow raised.

"Because it means they need us," I said firmly, my voice conversational but carrying. "The Conglomeration, they're using human forces. The Accordance is using us en masse. To reinvade Titan. Ken, you were right earlier. The only reason humans could have taken over these carriers and mutinied was because they were *building* them. We know how they work. Just a generation ago, under Arvani, we knew nothing about their technology. Now we build their ships and run them."

"Under their thumb," Amira said.

"For now. What happens after?" I said. "After the war is won? After we take all this knowledge back to Earth?"

“That’s a big if,” Ken said. “People like your parents are fighting for the independence movement. Arvani say we can explore home rule after the war, but if they won’t give it to us right now, when they need us the most, what makes you believe all that knowledge will be allowed back?”

“If we make sure it goes home,” I said. “If we’re hard as hell to stop. If we turn this war around. We’ll have the tools to demand a seat at the table from the Arvani.”

A loud chattering came from Shriek. He stood up and shook his wing hands, raising them up over his head. “I love your human enthusiasm,” he said, moving toward me. I pulled back slightly as the struthiform flapped wildly, blowing the air around me until grit from the floor stung my skin.

“Shriek!”

“It’ll be an amazing thing to die along with all of you,” Shriek said. “Defiant to the end! Well done.”

He left the room without his armor.

“Rockhoppers don’t shuck!” Zizi yelled after him. But Shriek ignored her.

“It *will* be a tough fight,” Ken said soberly. “Zeus is still down there. Waiting for us.”

I let out a deep breath. “He trained us. He knows our capabilities.”

“And we know his,” Amira said. “Another reason I think Anais is keen to have us in the first wave, and under his command.”

Ken stood up. “Captain Calamari is a walking corpse. A dead thing which just doesn’t know it’s dead yet.” He looked around the entire room. Anger was building inside him. “I used to think I understood the Arvani. I used to think I knew where and what was best for us all, what my training taught me. I’ve unlearned all this since the Darkside War. But I shall say this: No matter what happens in Shangri-La, I *will* have my revenge on Zeus. You all have heard this."

Ken's mood had bounced from despair through ennui and on into a general frustration at having his illusions about the Accordance refactored.

But now the old Ken was back.

"Damn squid's going to regret the day it ever heard of the Rockhoppers," Chaka shouted out.

"Hell, yeah." Patel smiled.

23

We blazed through the thick atmosphere of Titan like meteors, heat shields cherry red from the fireballs around us. Inside the jumpship, metal popped and creaked, the hull changing shape due to the intense pressures as the pilot shifted the angle of reentry.

"Helmets," Ken shouted.

I looked up and down the platoon as their faces were obscured by faceplates, suddenly anonymous except for the small nameplates.

Everyone was strapped in.

Everyone quiet, determined.

"Incoming!" the pilot, Gennadiy, warned on the common channel.

"I thought they took most of it out from orbit?" I leaned forward to look up toward the front. The nitrogen clouds flickered, lit up from inside by what looked like lightning.

"The Accordance heavy contingent stopped laying it down and moved out fifteen minutes ago," the pilot said. "Only the CPF carriers are in orbit now."

"What the fuck?" That wasn't supposed to happen. The fireball around us had faded. The pilot shuddered us into another curving turn down into the flashing clouds. "Where'd they go? Is it a retreat?" What were we flying down into without orbital support?

"No, not at that speed. They're repositioning," the pilot grunted.

"Where?"

"I don't know" was the annoyed answer. And then we banked hard again, knocking the breath out of me as the jumpship kept turning. We flipped upside down and the engines lit up. "They were supposed to knock out the anti-orbital weaponry, but we're getting a lot of fucking energy in the air."

We were pointed straight down at the ground and going all out.

"Holy shit!" Vorhis shouted.

"No point in dallying around!" Gennadiy shouted back.

Energy danced across the clouds, hopping from point to point and seeking us out. A dot far below us flared and then faded away in a cloud of debris. A concussive wave slapped the side of the jumpship, punching it twenty feet to the side and denting the hull. The craft began shaking hard enough that my vision blurred.

What sounded like rain pattered against the jumpship. We were diving through the remains of someone else.

Then came the flare-out. My armor kicked in to compensate against the sudden crushing force of the jumpship reversing thrust to prevent us from becoming a stain on the ground; it gripped my body and squeezed to keep blood up near my brain. My vision blurred, a rib cracked, and painkillers rushed in from the armor.

We struck the ground and slid for several hundred feet

through hydrocarbon-rich mud before coming to a stop.

My eyes wide, panting, I yanked myself out of the restraints. "Ken, Shriek, check the platoon status."

"We're way out of our LZ," Amira reported.

I was looking at the map overlay on my helmet already as well. "But we're inside the bowl." The pilot had just pointed down and done the insane thing of running all the anti-orbital weaponry in a straight shot. Pips and information from everyone else showed most of the CPF coming down on the other side of the hills. Or getting shot down on the final approach.

"Anyone else insane enough to try the direct approach?" I asked Gennadiy.

"A few of us decided on it when we realized the anti-spacecraft came back up," he said wearily. "They were getting shot down on final approach as well as in the deorbit. We figured, roll the dice, come in on rails, and skip the fancy dancing. We knew it was just a numbers game."

"Everyone's accounted for," Ken said.

"I'm looking at the maps and seeing heavy fire from these points. Those are the anti-orbital cannons we put in place; the Conglomeration moved some of them around," I said. There were smoking gaps in the hills where we had originally placed them. So, the Accordance had not taken the time to verify that they were melting actual emplacements. Just used the old coordinates and moved on. We showed up and were sliced and diced. "Amira? We get those knocked out, we create the space for any CPF trying to come over the hills to retake Shangri-La."

"Well, sitting here is going to be a bad decision in about a minute," Gennadiy said. "We have incoming. I need to get the hell out to safety."

I thudded my way forward. "Troll." Tons of gray armor plated hide came careening down the nearby slope toward us. "Everyone out!"

"We don't have artillery support here by ourselves," Ken said as I spun around. "Mortars aren't going to slow it down. Or hit it. It's moving too quickly."

"Move out!" I shouted, impatient. "Gennadiy, get out of here, I'm jumping. Amira, give orbital our position and bring in a laser, danger close."

I didn't have to ask twice; as the last of the platoon tumbled out, Gennadiy lit up and took the air. Ken and I jumped out, last of the group, and we were already a hundred feet off the ground in the seconds it took for Gennadiy to take off.

As I fell, I looked over at the approaching troll.

Big alien fucker. Multiple eyes. Something out of a bad dream. All sharp armor plates under that rhino-thick skin. Serrated claws.

"Run!" Ken shouted as he hit ice and dirt to find a squad waiting for us.

"Incoming in three . . . ," Amira said calmly on the common channel.

We bounced out like fleas, straining to push our armor to its limits.

". . . two . . ."

I was in midair and flying.

". . . one."

I curled into a ball and looked back behind me. The orange clouds above us split. Energy lanced down from above instead of leaping upward. The beam of focused energy boiled the ground where it struck, just to the left and forward of the troll that had skidded to a stop in an explosion of gravel. The world hummed and spat.

The beam adjusted course, Amira no doubt whispering instructions. It moved inexorably over the ground, leaving a great scar in its wake. The troll ran, but there was nowhere to hide. The beam of light swallowed it up with a sudden lurch of motion and then kept on moving.

There wasn't even a shadow.

I hit the ground in a sprawl and skidded to a stop on my belly. The orbital energy cannon snapped off. "How long for upstairs to recharge?" I asked.

"Ten minutes," Amira said.

I'd known that we wouldn't be able to walk up the hill behind an apocalyptic finger of energy from the carriers' anti-ship weapons being pointed downward, but I was still disappointed. At least, I thought, they were able to give us support and weren't under attack and needing their energy weapons for survival.

For now.

"Who else made it down into the bowl with us?" I asked.

"First Platoon, Charlie Company," Amira said.

"I saw some other pips scattered around on the tactical when we hit; did they link up with them?"

"No," Amira said.

They'd gone silent. I closed my eyes for a second. "Let's get to First Charlie."

We crunched across a field of dead crickets and toward a twenty-foot-long structure of cricket pieces that had assembled themselves into the form of a robotic worm. Half of its body was stuck inside the hole it had dug to try and surprise First Charlie from below ground.

The platoon had crash-landed in their jumpship and then

dragged it around to the front of the crater to use as a hasty shield as they'd dug in behind it.

"I didn't realize you guys were calling yourselves the Groundhogs," Zizi said on the common channel after we scooted in to join them behind the blackened remains of the canted jumpship. "You dig in any deeper here, you'll have a warren."

"Says the platoon hopping across the basin like fleas on crack to hide with us" came the annoyed retort.

"Zizi, shut up," I ordered. The atmosphere was still dancing with light stabbing out from the hilltops around us. The sky-scraper-sized anti-orbital weaponry that the Accordance had built here in Shangri-La was now being turned against them.

I used the live tactical map on my helmet to find the command pip nearby. Sergeant Natalie Cunningham sounded tired as she leaned in to look through helmets at me. She grabbed my shoulder. The armor-to-armor contact kicked in, giving us a secure line.

"Sorry about the chatter," I said.

"We're actually relieved you're in the shit stew with us," Cunningham said. "We thought we were going to be alone here. What's the plan?"

"Upstairs says we don't have to make a run uphill," Amira said. "It's still clear in orbit, so they can keep pointing down. We point out the new coordinates, they'll melt. Then we see what comes scurrying out. Anais is moving toward Shangri-La; they've rounded up a full company's strength."

"So, where are the Conglomerate ships? The Trojans? And where did the rest of the Accordance ships head to?" I asked.

"Lots of theories, lots of bullshit," Amira said.

I briefed Cunningham, picked some spotters, and sent out a squad each. Zhao took Bravo squad out. The basin had quieted. And the Conglomeration hadn't turned any heavy weaponry on the hills down into here.

Yet. I had Smalley take Alpha squad around our perimeter and start mining it.

We were keyed up, looking around, waiting for another wave of ground assault. But so far, it wasn't coming.

"Incoming," Amira muttered. The slopes behind us lit up. My helmet struggled to compensate as the anti-ship weapons from orbit reached down to the ground. The alien energy weapons under the beams of energy exploded, tortured matte-black and green shards flying across the basin.

No one had to be told to get low as debris larger than a jumpship struck icy gravel.

The light faded. "They're recharging," Amira said. "But that's a third of their capacity, easy."

The jagged tips of the hills were now soft and runny.

"Anais gives us ten minutes before he gets up the neutralized hill," Amira said. "Titan's cold enough, a crust will already be formed on the top. We'll have backup shortly."

"And we're going to need it," Zhao reported from cover against a ravine in one of the hills they'd dug into instead of coming back. "They're coming out of the ground."

I turned. Shielded covers were being blown off tunnel access points. Raptors moved out quickly to establish fields of fire. Then behind them . . . humans in surface suits. Hundreds of them boiled out.

"They're not in armor," Tony Chin said mournfully over the command channel. "All they have to fight with are small arms."

They were going to get slaughtered. I got on Shangri-La's civilian common channel. "This is Lieutenant Devlin Hart," I sent. "Please, you are unprotected and barely armed. Get back into the tunnels. The Colonial Protection Forces have come to ground to rescue you and take back Shangri-La. Remain below."

"The last thing we want is to go back to sitting under the thumb of Arvani lackeys," the response came. "Shangri-La is a free zone for humans. We've held elections, we've built a militia. Now we're going to make a stand."

"What is all that about?" one of Cunningham's soldiers asked.

"Conglomerate propaganda," Ken said with distaste.

"They're willing to die for it," I said. "Look." A wave of blue surface suits ran toward us.

"Lieutenant?" Cunningham asked on the common channel.

"Wait," I said.

The blue line grew larger. Bullets started to smack and splinter nearby rock. One pinged off my shoulder pad.

Someone, Rockhopper or First Charlie—it didn't matter—fired back. A clean shot, center mass. Blood exploded out of the back of one of the many blue suits and hung in the air as the figure stumbled and fell forward. The line continued to run right at us, more and more figures dropping, until they hit the mines.

Dirt fountained up, the ground thudded, and the wall of blue shattered. The dust settled to reveal them taking cover or turning back. Sixty bodies lay still in the scree between us and the main body of blue.

"Do you see that they're willing to die for freedom?" a familiar synthesized voice said on the common channel. "Do you understand what you can all get from the Conglomeration? Something the Accordance will never give you. Self-determination. Which means they're willing to face thugs like you to fight and keep it."

"Zeus," Ken said, voice dripping acid.

"I am willing," Zeus said, "to negotiate with the Conglomeration on your behalves. You can end further bloodshed. You don't have to keep cutting down so many, when you should all be sharing a common cause. The freedom of your kind."

"Where's the asshole?" I asked. "Zhao? What do you see? Do you see any Arvani out on the surface?"

"Spot five raptors, one Arvani in the mix at the center of all the blue. They're hanging close to the tunnels," Zhao reported. "Need us to punch in from the side?"

The moment they did, that I had a feeling Zeus would rabbit down into the tunnels. Somewhere, there'd be a plan to hole up for a siege. "No, this is an opportunity," I said. I looked around. "We need to lure him farther out."

I looked at the hole with the cricket boring machine slumped half out of it. A few of us could cram down in there with armor, right down the damn thing's gullet. "I have an idea," I said on the command channel. "To kill Zeus. But it will take just a few of us and leave us pretty vulnerable."

"I'm in," Ken said quickly.

"Me, too," Amira said.

"Okay, Zhao," I said. "I need a distraction to keep them looking your way while we get up to no good. Don't push too hard, just get Zeus's attention and then get holed up somewhere. Got it?"

"Yes sir!" she said enthusiastically.

24

We ripped our way through the heart of the cricket worm, wriggled our way deep inside, and then pulled the mechanical guts in after ourselves. Zhao was busy moving her squad around the back side of the attack, gaining their attention as she, Li, Chen, and Vorhis leapfrogged around, trying to get in a shot at Zeus or his raptor bodyguards.

"See the solar system," Amira said. "Visit exotic moons. Dig your way into the heart of a giant mechanical worm."

"Zhao? Break it off and get to safety," I ordered. "Smalley, tell Cunningham we're go."

"You sure?" Smalley asked.

"Do it," Ken snapped.

We listened to thuds as Cunningham and the rest of the Rockhoppers moved around the mines to engage. "You're right," Chin reported quickly. "Zeus is rushing us and moving them around behind us through the mines."

"Fall back," I ordered. "Don't forget to pass through the jumpship."

"We got it."

More thudding from around us as the two platoons stampeded back to their bolthole. Then more as they abandoned it and began to slowly retreat back toward the slagged hill. The sound of the firefight lessened as it moved away from us.

"Yeah, several of the raptors are clearing the jumpship," Zhao said. "He's not going to go himself, but he's moved farther away from the tunnel entrance. Think I spooked him."

"That's okay," I said. "We have the tunnel coordinates fixed. The moment Amira calls in the strike, we go all out for Zeus, okay, Zhao?"

"We're ready."

"Okay, Amira," I bit my lip. "Now."

I kicked clear and broke out of the cricket worm, pieces flying out as we ripped the entire thing apart in our haste. A nearby woman in blue fell to the ground writhing, a metal shard in her stomach. The blazing beam of light we'd called down from the sky was just fading away, and a puddle of lava boiled where the tunnel Zeus walked out of had been.

"There!" Ken shouted. I followed his armored finger and saw the scuttling form of the Arvani in armor running all out for the next nearest tunnel and then pulling up short as Zeus saw Zhao's squad cutting the escape off.

Amira and Ken were off, and I followed a second behind. Long arcing leaps through Titan's misty air, ignoring Zeus's hasty shots in our direction. The energy rifle could melt through our armor, but there were too many of us, moving too quickly, for Zeus to target. It sizzled and spat energy near me, but scored no direct hit.

"Ah, shit," Amira gasped.

"You okay?" I shouted. We were all locked on, firing in quick bursts. There was satisfaction in seeing the bullets strike and spark against Zeus's armor as we closed in, both squads converging. One of his legs cracked and leaked fluids, dragging behind him. Then another. Zeus slowed.

"I surrender," Zeus shouted on the common channel.

"Anais says capture only. No kill. We *cannot* kill Zeus," Amira said. "Direct order."

"I surrender!" Zeus shouted again on the common channel.

Ken slammed into Zeus, knocking the energy rifle away. Another shot and more of the alien's legs were immobilized.

"Raptors," Zhao said, sprinting right through us in the other direction.

But they too were skidding to a halt. They threw their weapons to the ground and froze. "They surrender as well," Zeus said.

Up at the top of the slagged hill, an entire company of CPF had crested and was pouring down the slope toward Shangri-La's basin. Over near the foothills, the blue surface-suit army straggled along but lost momentum as it saw the CPF numbers.

Two minutes later, it was done. The battle was over.

Ken dropped to his knees.

I couldn't hear anything; he'd cut his mic.

He started punching the ground, turning rock into gravel, and then gravel into dust.

"This," I said seven hours later, "is utterly ridiculous."

I was in an untouched jumpship just down from orbit. Ken, Amira, and I had gotten on; now it was flying a very quick thirty-second loop around the basin and coming right back toward where we had taken off. All the while, it was pursued by spherical camera drones.

“Cunningham should be in here. Chin, Zhao, and Smalley should be here,” I muttered.

The jumpship flared out, smacked dirt, and someone kicked the side door open.

“Do it smartly,” Anais ordered.

The three of us stepped up together and then hopped down to the ground. Our boots smacked Titan soil, and we marched toward the cloud of drones. The jumpship took off rapidly, mimicking clearing out of a hot LZ. Much like Gennadiy had just hours ago.

We burst out of the cloud, and Anais held up a hand. “Okay, that's all we need. The heroes of the Darkside War have done it again.”

He walked with us down into the tunnels and cycled through. We all flipped our helmets back. “They're still going room to room down there,” I said. “Couldn't this have waited?”

“No. Ninety percent of the base is cleared. And because we're going to run that clip out, with an announcement to those hiding in the rest of the base. They'll know who's arrived. And they're going to think twice, Devlin. This'll save lives.”

“And boost recruitment back on Earth,” Ken said.

And raise Anais's profile in the CPF, I thought.

“We've taken the corridor leading to the destroyed entrance of the weapons foundry,” Anais said, switching the subject away. “The Conglomeration was drilling through the debris we left in the way to get to it. Another half a day and they would have broken in and been able to arm people here against us. That attack on the surface would have gone a lot differently. These people might even have been showing up as our enemies elsewhere in the solar system, maybe even Earth. There are a hundred thousand people, here, Devlin. This was a great victory. We've retaken Shangri-La.”

"And what are we doing with all those people?" I asked. "They were willing to die for the Conglomeration up there."

"Not all of them volunteered to go topside. We detained those who did. The hostility is under control. Everyone else, we will have to monitor and build new understandings with," Anais said. "But we did it. We're back. We're here. Now, level three has a mess set up and some food dropped. Get fed, rejoin your platoon, and go get some rest. We have a lot of work ahead of us, Devlin. You and I will be talking to a lot of the leaders and people here. Regaining their trust."

Anais clapped me on the shoulder, armor smacking armor, and then turned down a corridor.

"I should have accidentally shot Zeus," Amira said. "Think Anais would be this cheerful if I'd done that?"

"PR wins the war," I said to her. "And he has his PR win, right? Let's go eat. And sleep."

I snapped out of my half-sleep and reached for my rifle. The distant explosion still echoed through the corridors, bouncing from wall to wall. Small arms fire chattered for a few seconds and then fell silent. My armor was on its back, ribs splayed, maw wide and patiently waiting. I lay next to it, head on a blanket against the armpit.

"What is it?" I asked, rubbing my eyes.

"Bomb." Amira was standing by the door in armor, on watch with Delta. "Good to know 'the hostility is under control' still," she said.

"We abandoned them here. The Conglomeration promised them freedom and seemed to give it. Then we came back. I don't think this is going to be easy," I said, voice scratchy from exhaustion.

“We’re the assholes,” Amira said.

“We’re the assholes.” I lay my head back down. Two more hours off watch. Then I’d be at the door by the bulkhead in full armor, waiting for something to happen.

“This is what they do,” Shriek said, speaking up.

“What?” I asked.

“Divide you. Get you to fight against each other. Give some of you freedom and riches beyond imagination to turn on yourselves. You’ll still lose it all. They’ll take it. Just like they did my world. You won’t rest until it’s time to flee between the worlds again. It’s nice out there in the dark. Quiet.”

“Like the Accordance did when they took Earth?” I asked.

“Shut up,” Amira said. “We can argue about which group of aliens is worse when we’ve had some sleep.”

25

Several squads had been tasked with clearing out the burned-out command center. The debris had been dragged out. Teams had scrubbed everything down. Techs were underneath stations hanging cables; someone with an arc welder occasionally lit the room up with sharp searing white light, their exaggerated shadows dancing along the walls. There were bustle and determined hurry everywhere I looked.

"Good to see us back up," Jun Chen muttered, looking around. We'd been called up to command. I'd picked Chen and Vorhis from Bravo squad to run with me.

Anais dwelled at the center of it all, the eye of the CPF hurricane.

But he didn't look all that calm.

In fact, for the first time since I'd ever met him, Anais looked flustered, exhausted, and worried.

"I didn't know you were in command of the operation," I said, joining him at the center of the calm. "I thought General Song would be here."

"The general didn't make it to ground," Anais said. "I ended up being the highest-ranked to land."

I searched my mind for something appropriate to say and came up blank. Instead, I half shrugged in my armor and grunted something vague.

Anais looked at me in the full armor. "Rockhoppers never shuck, right?"

"Yeah."

"I'm thinking that should go company-wide. Everyone in Shangri-La."

"Bombs got under your skin?" I asked. "Not enough people turn out waving flags to welcome the CPF back?"

Anais brushed that aside. "It's not *people* I'm worried about." He took a deep breath and then rubbed his forehead. Then he looked around as if worrying about anyone hearing him. Decided not to say anything. Then changed his mind again.

I'd never seen such an uncertain Anais before.

"Alien problem?" I prompted.

"The engineers and Zeus set charges in the heavy weaponry. We're vulnerable from above," Anais finally told me.

"We have orbit. Four carriers and their anti-ship weapons."

"What if we lose them?" Anais responded quickly. "I'm asking for replacements, my superiors are saying they won't be able to bring anything in."

Trouble in paradise. I suddenly realized that Anais was in the dark with the rest of us. "You don't know why the Accordance all left us in orbit, do you? They're shrooming you like the rest of us?"

"Shrooming?"

Too long spent with his tongue up Arvani assholes. I shook my head. "Putting you in the dark, feeding you shit? Like a mushroom."

"Oh." Anais nodded. "I wouldn't say I don't know what's happening. Come."

We walked across the control center to one of the old officers' cubicles. It had been quickly reinforced with heavy rebar welded into place to create a makeshift jail cell. Zeus sat inside, still in full armor. But his armored tentacles were all manacled to the walls.

"He has enough working environmental equipment to last a week or so if we give him some food here and there," Anais said. "He's talking to us."

"Talking?" I had to bite my lip. I wanted to shoot the Arvani in the faceplate, over and over again until it cracked and his water ran out and he choked in the air.

"They're not going to drop in any equipment to Titan," Zeus said, stirring to stand awkwardly despite the chains holding him in place. "Because they've already written off everything down here. No sense in throwing good after bad."

I whirled on Anais. "By putting this traitor piece of shit here in your command center, you're letting the enemy sit and whisper in your ear."

"You accused me of not knowing where the rest of the fleet went," Anais said. "Here's what I do know. Everything is on a fast burn for Saturn."

"Saturn?"

"But that's not the target. It's a fast burn and then a skip. They're going to whip around and keep going. Not coming back," Anais said.

"They're just going to leave us here?" I asked. "You truly believe that?"

That weight he'd been carrying. I could see what it was. "I think we were a diversion," Anais said wearily.

"You were," Zeus boomed. "There are too many Conglomeration even on Titan for you to do more than hold Shangri-La for a while before being overrun. They are underground, in other Conglomerate bases. Once the humans here agreed to terms, most of the invasion forces left. I was enough, with my bodyguards."

I glanced over scornfully. "What, you're telling us this out of a desire to help?"

"To assist myself, yes," Zeus said, large octopus-like eyes wide behind the watery glass. "If what Anais says is true, nothing else matters other than my need to get off Titan."

"So, it is self-preservation?" I raised an eyebrow, dubious.

Zeus shook his shackles. "Titan is lost. Saturn is lost. It is now time to poison the reef to keep it from your enemies. To leave the stain of death upon it forever so that it will be tasted in all the currents nearby, so that all understand what happens when your territory is taken from you."

Anais and I both moved closer to the welded rebar as one. "What do you mean?" I asked. "What happens next?"

"You've already seen it, humans. You've seen what happens to the worlds that are taken from the Accordance. It is broadcasted to you all. The Conglomeration do what they can, but they die in the plagues and horror the Accordance unleash so that the Conglomeration *cannot* use those worlds against the Accordance."

If I wasn't locked into full armor, I would have wanted to sit down. "The Accordance?"

"If we lose a world," Zeus explained, "we unleash biological bombs. Weapons that won't pop and fizzle in a small little area. We unleash something that will destroy *everything*. If the Accordance fleet has left you, if it is burning for Saturn, then everything in the Saturn system dies.

Taking Titan, that was to get the Conglomeration to pay attention here."

"We drop down. We kick things up, and then we go back up to the carriers and run away," I said. "That's how you'll know if the squid's right. If we get ordered back upstairs."

Anais was leaning against the bars, holding himself up on them. "Would they bomb everyone down here? After we leave?"

"The Conglomeration is here," Zeus said simply.

I turned to Anais. "How do you like your masters now?"

"Now is not the time for treasonous talk," he said wearily.

"*When* is it the time?" I asked.

"The traitor is messing with our heads. You were right at the start," Anais said, straightening up. "I shouldn't have chained him up here. Or even talked to him. There are Conglomeration that will be counterattacking. We need to prepare for *that*."

"You have just hours before the call. You know the fleet is swinging close to Saturn," Zeus said on the common channel. "You need to start evacuating now. Get yourselves, and me, well clear of here."

"Get back to your platoon, Lieutenant," Anais ordered, face hardening as he ignored the Arvani. "And stay armored up."

"Rockhoppers don't shuck," I said.

Anais looked at Vorhis and Chen. "They good?"

"Rockhopper solid," I said.

"Leave them guarding Zeus. They don't listen to anything he says. They don't let anyone talk to Zeus."

"You're splitting up my platoon?" I wasn't happy with that.

"I need everyone else putting things back together or sweeping tunnels. I need two on Zeus that have seen the fight."

"I'll do it. But you called me here because I know Zeus," I said. "You wanted that expertise. We trained with Zeus. We fought Zeus. You wanted my opinion. Here it is: The squid is right. You want advice from your heroes of the Darkside War? Get prepared for the worst, not just dug in."

26

I looked at Amira. "It's happening all over again," I said. Some sort of sick, bizarre déjà vu. "We're going to have to abandon Titan. This was all bullshit."

Ken stood up in his armor, a complete look of horror on his face. He looked as sick as I knew I must have. The three of us were in the platoon's chosen barracks, but the squads were out on tunnel duty. Amira and Ken were waiting for me.

Amira didn't look surprised. Or much of anything. She just nodded. "Okay. We're evacuating again?"

"Amira, are you even listening to me?" I snapped.

"Yes. We're abandoning Titan. It's all bullshit." Amira looked from Ken to me. "What?"

"The carriers, the jumpships, we can't get everyone off Titan." I explained it slowly, as if to a child.

Amira sighed. "You studied history, Devlin. Ken, you trained for this. You have to know this happens all the time. This is fucking war. Armies abandon positions. They retreat. They come back. They protect. They abandon. They win. They lose."

“The Accordance is going to destroy everything so that the Conglomeration can’t have it,” I told her.

“They’re salting the fields,” Amira said.

“*We’re* the fields.”

She looked at me. I was wrong; there wasn’t a blankness there. There was an intensity in her silvered eyes. “We always were the resources they were fighting over. That they wanted utter control of. Now we know: The Accordance would rather destroy us than not control us. What does that tell you about your dreams of Earth rule?”

That if they won against the Conglomeration, they wouldn’t gratefully hand us anything.

I stalked around the barracks. “We have to think of something. We have to start getting them off planet now. We need a plan to show Anais so that we’re ready when—”

Armor blared an incoming all-call.

“All platoons to rally point three.” Anais sounded tired, his voice cracking slightly. “Situation Feather. Jumpships incoming.”

Situation Feather. Carry only weapons and ammo. Get to your predetermined point within the next ten minutes. Get there alert and weapons hot.

No, I moaned to myself. No. We were abandoning Shangri-La.

We had to pause. We had to think of something.

“Jun Chen, Alpha Company Third Platoon to anyone listening: Command is under attack. I have wounded. I need assistance now!”

Without a word, we grabbed our weapons and skidded out. I slammed into the wall across from the barracks, shattering rock and leaving gravel in my wake as I sprinted up the tunnel and back toward Command. Ken and Amira rocketed along with me, careening off turns as they raced with me.

"Chen, report!" I shouted.

Nothing from Chen. The chatter of gunfire from up the tunnel turned into loud smacks as bullets bounced off my armor. We ducked behind bulkheads.

"Human," Ken said. "Lead."

"Chen!" I shouted. "How many do you think?"

Amira responded. "Judging from gunfire, four, in the hallway between us and Command."

"Cameras?"

"They knocked them out, I'm blind," Amira said.

What surprises were in store?

"I'll take point. Amira, cover. Ken, right behind me. Tight."

"Got it."

I swung around cover and charged. Acting as a shield for Ken in case there was something more heinous than bullets waiting for us. Conglomerate energy weapons.

The first man with a submachine gun dropped, still backpedaling for cover. His blood splattered against the rock wall. The second screamed as her weapon exploded in her hands, a snap shot from Ken. "Stay behind!" I ordered.

Through and into the command center. "Take left," I said. I swept the room, Ken splitting off from me to sweep left. The emergency lights flickered, illuminating bodies.

Movement. I snapped my rifle up, and two shots cracked. Two bodies slumped forward, grenades of some kind in their hands. "It's Chen; don't shoot!" She stepped out from the shadows without armor, a pair of pistols in hand as she kicked the grenades aside. "That clears the command center."

"Clear," Ken whispered on the command channel.

"Coming," Amira said.

"Where's your armor?" I asked Chen.

“Fucked.” She pointed at it. A dissolved hunk of twisted material lying face down on the floor.

“Vorhis?” Ken asked. Amira stepped into Command, covering the way we’d entered.

Chen pointed at another burned-out chunk of armor. “Inside. Didn’t get out in time. Screamed a lot. The grenade sticks and starts eating away at the armor. Conglomerate. I got out of the line of fire and shucked while they were cracking Zeus out.”

“Which direction?” Ken asked calmly.

“They’re going topside,” Chen said. She staggered a bit. I saw blood dripping from her side.

“Shriek, get up here or send someone. Chen’s wounded. Vorhis is down. There may be more in the command center.”

“I regret having known their names,” Shriek said.

“Not the time, Shriek,” I growled.

“I have cameras,” Amira said. “I have Zeus. Topside.”

“Chen?” I asked.

“Go,” she hissed.

“Shriek’s on the way,” Ken shouted back at her as we followed Amira back out into the tunnels and then up onto the plains.

“Fourth has eyes on them,” Amira said. “They’re up on one of the slagged sections of hill. Zeus and three humans are running hard.”

“Yeah, I’ll bet,” Ken said. “But he’s not going to be running too fast after you destroyed his joints.”

“No, they’re helping him across the ground. What are they running to?” Amira asked. “That’s what I’m trying to figure out.”

“If Zeus wants to commit suicide on the surface, I’m happy to help.” Ken leaped out front.

“Hold back, let’s encircle,” I ordered. “They might have more of those grenades. And we’re outside here. Get Fourth down off the hill, Amira.”

“That’s a polite negative from them,” she said. “Anais’s orders are still in effect for falling out to the rally point. Jumpships are incoming. Now.”

I glanced up. The waspish shapes of jumpships were breaking through the thick clouds and circling overhead like mechanical buzzards.

We had air support. Orbital cannon. What the fuck was Zeus doing out here.

“Crickets!” Ken shouted.

A swarm of mechanical crickets burst out of the ground near the foothills ahead of us. Behind them, through the thick, rapidly spinning cloud, I saw the great maw of another worm-like cricket wriggling free of a freshly chewed hole. The cricket swarm had come in behind it and now surged around the worm.

“That is a large cloud,” I said.

“If Zeus gets into that tunnel, leading who knows where, and they plug it behind him, you know we’ll never see Zeus again,” Ken shouted.

“We can’t face off against that many out here,” Amira said, slowing down.

But Ken charged on, heading for the edge of the cloud that swirled around Zeus and the three people in surface suits.

“The swarm’s not engaging us, just defending,” Amira noted.

Ken, ahead of us, pounded toward the roiling boundary of crickets.

“Devlin?” Amira asked.

“Clear us a path, Amira,” I said.

“I can’t kill them all.”

"I know; just get us in there." I sped up, struggling to get to Ken as he hit the wall just as a wave of crickets fell out of the air in front of him, struck by the beam of Amira's EPC-1 at the apex of one of her long jumps. The world around us darkened, light blocked by thousands of small bodies whirling above.

"I'm going to run into the tunnel after I grab him," Ken said, speaking for the first time. The three human escorts spun to attack him, but they were no match for Ken. He bounced and jigged around them, leaving their still bodies on the ground.

I ran through a hailstorm, crickets smacking armor as Ken and I surged through into the eye of the mechanical hurricane. "Can you bring down orbital on us when I call it out?" I asked Amira. Crickets peeled off to follow us, a levitating arm of dark swirling material. But we pushed the armor to its edge as we smacked into Zeus.

"The tunnel, now!" Ken shouted. Ken yanked the Arvani off his tentacles, hugging him to his chest like a prize and not slowing down a bit.

I spun around as I jumped and threw grenades out behind us and then started firing as I flew backward down into the tunnel, not knowing what I was going to hit. The thick, chittering cloud boiled and swerved to follow me in. The large earth-eating cricket machine stirred to life, raising itself up and opening its mouth and then jamming rotating bits into the tunnel head.

"Amira: Fire! Fire! Fire!" I shouted, smacking into the dirt and bouncing. I struggled to keep facing the mouth of the tunnel. Our fire chipped away at the large machine's hungry mouths but did nothing to slow it down as it wriggled toward us.

The ground thumped and shivered. Rocks tumbled and fell down, knocking me aside with their impact.

But the machine kept coming. The orbital energy had probably cut it in half and killed all the crickets outside, but whatever was left came for us.

"Back, back!" I kept fire on it, sparking away.

"Grenades!" Ken warned. Three of them sailed right over my head into the gaping, serrated mouths. I shielded my faceplate as the explosion ripped chunks of crickets out into the air and clattering against us.

It still came at us.

"I'm out," Ken said.

"We're going to have to run," I said.

"And where does this tunnel lead?" Ken asked. "Into more Conglomeration? I'll stand. At least Zeus will die before I do, and that is a victory I'll take."

We stepped back some more, weapons chattering and chipping parts off the machine as it struggled closer. Then it jerked, ripples of motion randomly dancing around the chewing mouths. It slowed, randomly spasming, until it came to a complete stop just ten feet from us.

Several explosions rippled through it, cricket debris falling down from the roof of its throat. Hot fireballs belched from the mouth. Amira kicked through its gullet and pointed her EPC-1 up above her. She fired twice and the machine stopped squirming.

She looked around. "Clear."

We surrounded Zeus. Ken pulled the magazine out of his rifle, checked it, and then rammed it back home. "I have been waiting to do this for a very long time," he said to Zeus on the common channel.

Amira took a step back.

"Ken," I tentatively started, not sure what I was going to say next.

"We kill him here. Say it happened in the chaos," Ken said.

"I've been blocking any transmission on the suits," Amira said. "This is a dead zone. No one will know for sure what happened in here."

"We execute someone, we're stepping over a line," I warned.

"We were considering running away from the CPF up in the Trojans," Amira said. "I think, after all we've seen, we're no longer walking within the lines."

"He deserves to die," Ken said. "For what he did. To all of them back on Icarus Base."

If he wanted to do this, I wasn't going to be able to stop him. I wasn't going to raise my rifle on him. Not Ken, who'd had my back through hell. Hell with aliens thrown in. I bit my lip and waited with a sick feeling in my stomach.

"STOP!" Anais shouted on the common channel. He scrambled over the remains of the tunneling cricket machine in a blue surface suit. "Do not execute the Arvani officer! We take him prisoner back with us. Arvani will put him on trial."

Ken stared down the barrel of his rifle at Zeus's large, liquid eyes.

"That's a direct order," Anais said.

"I'm sorry," Chen said, limping up behind him in a similar surface suit and holding a rifle. "Couldn't hold him back any more."

Something like a howl came over the command channel. Ken pushed his rifle forward until it tapped Zeus's visor. Then he yanked it back and slung it over his shoulder. He grabbed one of Zeus's tentacles and dragged the Arvani along with him through the slagged mechanical entrails of the cricket machine.

"It's time to get on the next jumpship up," Anais ordered. "Each of you, off Titan now. You're not staying behind to assist. I want you on the first wave. Got it?"

We trudged out of the tunnel and into a burned-out crater above where the crickets had once swirled. Jumpships were lined up inside Shangri-La. Armored CPF waited in lines to get aboard. Burn for orbit. Leave all this behind.

The common channel filled with chatter. People begging for spaces aboard the jumpships. I took a light hop up over our group and scanned the tunnel exits. Thousands of people in blue surface suits were spilling out onto the surface and trying to get to the ships. They were being held back by armored lines of CPF.

"We can't do this," I said to Anais. "You know this is *wrong*."

"Last night, half of those blue suits were trying to bomb us. Now they're begging to go with us? How many of them are Conglomerate spies? How many will turn on us?" Anais stayed close to Zeus, keeping an eye on Ken. "Listen, we've been able to create a list. We have room for a few thousand. We'll take the most qualified with no hint of Conglomerate sympathies."

"Everyone needs them," I told him. "The Conglomeration *and* the Accordance, they came to this system in just a handful of ships. They both need us. They're fighting over us. And we need them too. These people are our future. They know Accordance and Conglomeration technology. Leave them behind, we leave human survival behind, Anais. It's surrender. If we lose these minds, even if they hate us, we lose *everything*."

"We don't have the space," Amira said. "I hate to argue their side. But what's your play?"

We all stopped in front of the closest jumpship.

"You're not in charge here!" Anais shouted. "Get on board!"

"I can't do that," I said. "It's unacceptable."

"This is going to be a hell of a lot more than unacceptable, Lieutenant." Anais hit the front of my armor. "I'm going to charge you with mutiny if you don't get the fuck aboard now! You have your orders!"

I took a deep breath. "Since when is merely following orders an excuse to leave tens of thousands to die? What are we fighting for if we become no different than the things we're fighting? We have to be better than them."

Three rifle shots made me jump. Anais spun around. He looked down at the slumped body of Zeus by his feet and then up at Ken, who was slipping his rifle back under an arm.

"What have you just done, Awojobi?" Anais asked, a hushed shock in his voice.

"He's right," Ken said, sounding totally at peace. "This is mutiny." Ken reached forward with an armored hand and flicked Anais in the temple. Anais slumped to the ground, and Amira reached out to catch him before he could hit it.

"Is he dead?" I asked, dazed.

"Knocked out." She stood up, holding a slumped Anais in her arms. His arms hung loose in the air, and his legs hung over her forearm. "Now what?"

I stared at them both.

27

Amira shifted and slung Anais over her shoulder. "Okay, boss, what now?" she repeated.

"You're looking at me?" I was still in shock. "Me? I didn't . . . I mean, there are other people in charge. We need to go and talk to them. Create a plan."

"Talk. Plan." Amira swept her hands around. "The jump-ships are *here*. Armor's on the ground. This is happening now. What's next, Devlin?"

The line of armor up near the tunnel exits folded back several paces, overwhelmed by the sheer numbers pressing against it. The secondary line pulled weapons. The babble on the common channel was overwhelming. A thunderstorm of voices and panic. The crowd could sense something wrong in the air.

Everyone in armor would get on aboard those ships.

Everyone in blue would stand on the plains of Shangri-La and look upward as the ships burned their way up into the atmosphere and left them behind.

Again.

I took a deep breath. "I don't have the rank."

"It's falling apart anyway," Ken said. "Right in front of us. Command structure."

"Armor's fighting over who gets on the first wave," Amira said.

Ken raised both his hands. "Do you have a plan?"

"No." I shook my head in my helmet.

"All of this is happening because you're pissed off that this is unjust," Amira snapped.

"Because there *has* to be a way to save them." I looked out at the growing crowds. "Because there has to be a better way. Because this is a waste."

"Then *how*?" Amira asked.

"I don't know!" I looked around. "I've been thinking about it. I can't stop trying." We just didn't have *time*.

"Take a moment. What tools do we have?" Ken asked.

"The only damned tool I have is that everyone seems to know who we are. And what good is that?"

"It means everyone will listen to you. The hero of Icarus Base," Ken said. "Yes. Yes. How do we use this?"

"I fucking hate that shit," I said.

"No. You're going to embrace that shit," Ken insisted. "You're going to own it. We must use any weapon we have. What is it Anais said?"

"PR," I blurted.

"PR," Ken repeated. "What do we do with it? Is it enough for us to take command of everything on Shangri-La?"

"I've spent all this time struggling to control just a platoon, Ken. Without your help, I would never have been able to handle all this," I told him. Maybe, I realized, for the first time. "Taking control of all this?"

And then, I thought, losing so many more.

So many more lives that would be my fault when they died.

It was easier to fight and complain when Anais was in charge. It was easier to hate the decisions. Now Ken had made a decision that put me in charge. Now the problems could be mine.

Leadership wasn't just giving orders, though. It was listening. "We're not going to take command of Shangri-La. That's not my place. I can't usurp the chain of command. But there is something else I can do."

"Yes?"

"It's time to leverage the one thing we have that no one else has," I told Ken. "You're right. Get me to the command center. Amira, I need you with us. I need you to boost signals."

"What are you planning to do?" she asked.

"Use our greatest asset to save as many lives as we can," I said.

28

Amira, with Anais still thrown over her shoulders like a bright blue fur coat, moved around the command center, checking equipment over. The emergency lights still flickered, bodies had been pulled to a side of the room, and everyone had left to get to rally points. We'd forced our way through angry blue surface suit crowds to get here.

"It's not time to think about taking over something," I said. "Because then I'm only someone giving the orders. Just different orders. And then my reach is limited to whoever is on the ground. We need to think bigger."

"Bigger?"

"It isn't enough to just have different orders. We need to offer a chance. For all of us. Amira, I want this to go out everywhere. As far as you can boost."

"Titan-wide?"

"Orbit. Beyond. Human forces in the system. Up the quantum-entangled comms, throughout CPF. Anywhere you can get it. Conglomeration. Common channels. Anything and everything."

Amira had stopped. "Everything?"

"Everything," I repeated firmly.

There were moments of clarity. Like when I had crouched in front of a child during the riots outside the acting president's mansion in Richmond to stop him from being shot at. Or deciding to fight back against the Conglomeration at Icarus Base. Moments where I knew what I was doing was right. Regardless of what made sense, or what I'd been told to do.

Stand tall, let history judge. Even if it judges harshly. Something my dad said.

Though he would barely have understood any of the decisions I'd made since leaving to join the CPF. To save his life. My mother's. To buy everyone back home time to live, survive, and move on.

Amira pointed at me. "I'll amplify anything you say on the common channel." She held up four armored fingers.

A babble of noise swept through all the various channels, my head tracking them all automatically thanks to the neural link to the armor.

"Mayday, mayday, mayday . . ."

Emergency squawk.

Two armored fingers.

The squeal of digital code transmission over common analog channels.

And Amira closed her fist.

Silence.

I stood still for a long moment. Then took a deep breath. "To anyone who can hear this: I am Devlin Hart. You may know me as one of the survivors of Icarus Base. I am currently making an emergency call from Shangri-La Base to anyone who can hear me. We need your assistance. We need it now.

"There are almost a hundred thousand citizen contractors here on the base. They are engineers, workers, builders. They are us. They're our future. Our hope. Our brothers in arms. And the Accordance has ordered us to abandon them *yet again* as we pull out. But this time, it means certain death. The Accordance is about to unleash a weapon to destroy everything on Saturn and its moons. And anything, or anyone, left behind will suffer.

"So, I'm calling on any- and everyone with the capacity to get down from orbit and back, please come. CPF soldiers, you're being ordered to get aboard jumpships. I'm begging you, get aboard only three at a time, and give everyone else a space. Make the ships come back again and again. Pilots, make more than one trip. Carriers, send everything you have. We cannot leave people here to die like that.

"I swear to you. I will be the last person to leave Shangri-La Base."

I looked over at Amira. She nodded. "Okay, that's it."

Responses began to trickle in. Unauthorized broadcast. Cancel that. Everyone was being ordered into the ships. But there was back chatter. Confusion. It rippled out and around. I could hear my squad leaders checking in with each other as they moved through CPF platoons, moving to convince others this was the right action.

"Come on," said Ken. "We need to get up there and help."

Amira gave a thumbs-up. "Chaos is spreading. I'm hearing ships detaching to come down against orders. Command is ordering them back into their berths."

The first wave of jumpships was already leaving when we got to the surface. On the ground: armor. Lots of it.

"Okay," I ordered. "Start pinging the incoming ships, find out how many. Then let's make lines. We have a sense for how many we can cram into each jumpship. Mark every group, and then as they land, assign each group a ship. We board fast. They burn for orbit. Drop them off. Come back down."

"If the Conglomeration attacks now, a lot more of us will die. Soldiers that could have gotten away in that first wave," someone said on the common channel. "Lieutenant Hart, you better fucking hope they don't start picking us off."

"They'll be running," Shriek shouted. "Now that Hart broadcast the Accordance plans. They likely suspected it, but now they'll know for sure."

I swallowed. "I'm worse than a mutineer. I'm an Accordance traitor now. What death does the Accordance have for a traitor?"

"They were willing to destroy every life here," Ken said. "Without qualm. How can they expect loyalty if they're willing to toss our lives aside?"

"Some humans who were helping shuttle other Accordance resources around are coming down now," Amira said.

Seven jumpships burst through the clouds over the plain and landed. CPF troops got aboard, three to each ship, packing blue surface-suited people aboard as tightly as they could. People were lying down on top of each other, holding onto anything they could.

"Any Conglomeration out there?" I asked one of the pilots, standing in front of the cockpit windows and waving.

"You Hart?" he asked.

"Yes. Any Conglomeration?" I repeated.

"Yeah, we've seen some cricket swarms. But they're leaving us alone. Boogying for orbit. Rats off a sinking ship, man."

Two CPF soldiers shoved people on board and then struggled to close the doors. Gravel and ice spattered my armor as the jumpship roared off.

Anais groaned and struggled to sit up. Amira dropped him to the ground. "Anyone have zip ties?" she shouted.

Ken got down on the ground next to her. "I do," he said, and then proceeded to hog-tie Anais.

"What are you doing?" Anais asked groggily. He yanked at the zip ties and looked around. Then he wriggled onto his back to watch the jumpships punching for orbit far overhead.

"Good morning, sir. Nice to have you back," Amira said cheerfully, leaning over him.

Anais stared at her, rightfully suspicious at Amira's sudden sunny use of formal protocol.

"Hart, you're trying to evacuate everyone," Anais said fuzzily. He looked over to me. "Get me off the ground and out of these restraints. I will try to figure out how to fix this if you do it. Now. You have no fucking clue how deep the shit is going to get on this."

"It's the right call," I said softly.

Anais looked to Ken next. "Awojobi, you of all people should understand how horrible this decision is. You're committing treason."

"Me, of all people," Ken said. "I gave my all to the Accordance. My family gave their all. I came here to protect them. To protect them and stop the Conglomeration. Now I see how easily the Accordance would leave them to die."

"There are many examples of countries in war turning their guns on things the enemy might come back to use. This is not sports. There is no honor here in war, only winning or losing," Anais snapped. "And thanks to you, we'll be losing CPF soldiers today."

"We lose if we leave these people to die," I said. "Maybe not today. But we will lose."

"You've read too much indigenous literature. You think

there is honor, that there are rules, in battle? It is a human construct, Lieutenant Hart. And you are caught in the middle of a war between aliens with alien values."

"Maybe. Or maybe that's PR we tell ourselves to commit horrors in war. No one is ever fond of hearing the words 'I was just following orders' when it all settles out. I learned that from reading too much indigenous literature. I think there is only life. The life we lead. And the choices we make in that life define it. So, I don't know if I'm going to live through this, but I know I'm going to make the right fucking choice, Anais. I'm going to save as many lives as I can."

"You can't save them all," Anais said.

The next wave began to circle down out of the clouds. Jumpships darkening the skies.

And yet there were far too few of them to save the surging, panicked crowds of blue. Anais was right. I couldn't save them all.

How many more trips could I get away with before some Accordance officer reasserted control over this and stopped it? Before fear gripped the soldiers on the ground who wanted to get away?

As ships hit the ground, I picked up Anais, slung him over my shoulder, and walked him over to the nearest ship. I packed him in with all the other blue surface suits. "Cut him loose when you get to orbit," I ordered. Then I looked at Amira and Ken. "You two should go."

They didn't answer. They shoved more surface-suited people aboard until the inside of the ship was a mess of limbs and people standing shoulder to shoulder, and then shut the doors on them.

The jumpships began dusting off one by one and following each other back up to orbit.

We were alone on the ground again.

"How many off the ground?" I asked. "Anyone able to keep a headcount?"

"The carriers are saying six thousand, if you include this lift," Amira said.

Didn't seem like enough. But considering that the rally points had only been set up to lift a couple thousand troops back to orbit, it was impressive.

But not impressive enough.

The ground shook. "What's that? Are we expecting that?"

"It's coming from thirty miles away," Amira said. "Not local."

How the hell did she do that? "Anyone on the hills?"

"I can bounce up," Min Zhao said. "I'm close."

"Yeah, let's get some eyes on the hills." The shaking increased, knocking loose a few boulders on the hills. Then it stopped. We all stood around nervously.

"There it is," Amira said.

The form rising up above the hills was familiar. The matte-black jellyfish shape of a Conglomerate starship. And even though it was thirty miles away, it was *big*.

"Everyone get into the tunnels," I shouted. "Or take cover."

We'd stood against one of these on the Earth's moon. I wasn't sure what we could do against it here. We'd gotten lucky that first time.

The alien starship, loaded with an overwhelming Conglomerate force that had attacked us to take Shangri-La, shook off the last pieces of Titan from its shell as it accelerated for orbit, followed by a swarm of crickets that surrounded it like an ominous black mist.

The clouds swallowed it.

"We're no longer *the* tourist destination we once were," Amira said.

+ + + +

The next wave of jumpships came in aggressively. Ten ships that circled around the air above the basin, sniffing and hunting for something.

Me.

They surrounded the three of us and Accordance energy cannon dropped from their bellies, tracking our suits.

Twenty CPF in armor jumped the last hundred feet to the ground and fanned out toward us, weapons drawn.

Lana Smalley jumped in. "What do you need us to do?"

I stepped forward. "We need those jumpships to touch down and take people back to orbit."

"Our orders are to take Lieutenant Devlin Hart, Sergeant First Class Ken Awojobi, and Sergeant Amira Singh into custody and get to orbit," their commander stated. "That is a direct order from Colonel Anais. There will be no more lifts."

"There have to. There are still over ninety thousand people down here. Hell, most of the CPF soldiers are still on the ground," I protested.

"Something you'll have to answer for," the commander said grimly. "But there's no time left, Lieutenant. The Accordance missiles are incoming. There will be no more jumpships to Titan after these ten."

"Then take someone else instead of us. I said I would be the last one standing here. I will keep that promise."

Amira very casually shifted her EPC-1 forward.

"HELLO, DEVLIN HART," a voice boomed on all frequencies. "I HAVE HEARD YOUR MESSAGES. KNOW THAT YOU ARE KNOWN TO US, AND THAT I AM KNOWN TO MANY AS HAPPILY SLINGSHOT, AND I AM HERE TO ASSIST YOU."

29

The Pcholem descended from the clouds with the grace of a large sea creature slipping through murky waters and then lowered itself toward the valley. Its extended invisible fields broke the tips of the hills as it slid overhead and then settled down carefully between us all.

Fleeing CPF soldiers trying to get out from underneath bounced away like tiny fleas, only to find themselves frozen in midair and gently pulled toward the center of the alien starship.

"DEVLIN HART, SO PLEASED TO MEET YOU. COME TO ME!"

Amira raised her hands. "I don't think it's a good idea to ignore the orders of a giant interstellar starship, do you?"

I looked around. "Boost me on the common, if you can."

"On it," she said.

"Everyone, get to the Pcholem starship. Now!" I ordered.

The words had their effect. The tide of blue surface suits broke for Happily Slingshot. And mixed in with them, the dark spots of CPF armor springing their way aboard as well.

"Come on, you can't get back aboard the jumpships now," I shouted. The waspish shapes were turning and heading back for orbit. "Get aboard now, you live. Arrest me later."

The soldiers slung their weapons and ran with us.

How fast could ninety thousand people board a starship hovering just centimeters above Titan's icy, gravelly surface?

Five minutes for everyone to get within the Happily Slingshot's reach. Five minutes before it decided to leave.

Happily Slingshot rose into the air. People shouted in surprise as they were picked up by nothing, held in the living starship's embrace as it took to the air. The arrow-like shape of the ship's core flattened. Spars reached out from over and underneath like fast-growing ribs.

The shields flared as we spiraled up into the clouds, shoving them aside.

"THERE IS LITTLE TIME," Happily Slingshot said over all the common channels, drowning everyone out. "WHEN I HEARD THE CALL, WE ALL REALIZED I WAS CLOSEST. I RACED. I FEARED I WOULD BE TOO LATE. NOW I REJOICE THAT WE ARE ALL MET."

A struthiform shape in armor struggled through the crowds of people standing on what looked like air, and looking down two miles to the tops of Titan's thick clouds, to embrace me. It was Shriek. "Your fame grows wide and far, human." He pulled back his helmet and fluttered his wings. "You did it. You saved all these people."

In the distance, broaching another cloud, another massive jellyfish shape swam for the purple line of orbit.

"ABOMINATION," Happily Slingshot shouted. "I SEE YOU." But the Pcholem did nothing more than shout at it, veering off away from it to keep climbing.

“WE APPROACH ORBIT,” Happily Slingshot announced. “WHERE SHALL I BE TAKING YOU, DEVLIN HART?”

That . . . was a good question. I looked at Ken and then Amira. “Thoughts?”

“Earth,” they both said. “Get them back to Earth.”

Earth. Where they could pass on what they’d learned. Spread more Accordance technology out to our own scientists. These were going to be the seeds of something new.

I wasn’t just a kid buying time for my parents now. I was going to make a decision about how to sow the seeds of the Earth that would come after this war. And I had to assume, I had to plan, as if we were going to make it.

Besides, we didn’t have supplies or resources to survive long. Even on the Pcholem.

“Earth,” I said to Happily Slingshot. “We’re going to Earth.”

I slid my helmet back and took a breath of fresh air. “The Accordance has me now, though. When we arrive, they’ll have me arrested.”

Shriek put a wing hand around my shoulder. “But it does not, my human friend. You are far from their grasp now. Even going back."

“What do you mean?” Ken asked.

“You know the Pcholem need people that work for them, to help build and equip them with technology. Upgrades. Their trade networks span many stars. And when they found the Arvani, swimming around in their oceans, they reached down from orbit and gave them so much. They were impressed, you see. The way they were able to build their suits to get onto land. To develop their technology despite being in the water. A feat unparalleled! But in exchange, the Arvani tried to rule them. The war ended with Pcholem withdrawing all. But when the Conglomeration came, and then the Arvani became useful again. The Accordance, an alliance between those who would be swept away. Born out of need. But do not think the Pcholem bow to Arvani. They tolerate them."

"So, you are telling me we are safe if we stay right here?" I said. We were over Titan now. The world a sphere below us. Explosions dotted the night sky below us. Accordance missiles, scouring the planet.

"As safe as anyone can be against the implacable nature of the Conglomeration," Shriek said. "And I think maybe, just maybe, there is a small possibility you might live, Devlin. You'll still see your world burn, of that I have no doubt. But maybe there will still be humanity afterward. Because the Pcholem respect what you just did. Your stand for individual lives. They will be your allies. Do not mistake me: I will not be memorizing all the names of the people in your platoon. But I do not regret knowing yours."

I stared down at the moon below as it receded faster and faster from us. Happily Slingshot had turned on the after-burners, or whatever the alien equivalent was.

"There is a dark stain spreading across that surface," Shriek said. "It will melt anything alive it comes across."

For the next hours, as we passed Saturn's rings, we could see the explosions rippling all throughout the gas clouds of the giant planet. Tiny, from our perspective. But each one lethal with self-replicating cellular violence spreading on the winds.

"Your home world," I asked Shriek. "Was it like this? Was it the Accordance, like Zeus said?"

The struthiform never took his eyes off Saturn. "Did we destroy our nest to save ourselves from the raptors? To gain a little more time to live? Would we have done that to gain a place in the exodus? What rapacious creatures would we be if this were true? Would a life of service to healing even begin to count against such a horror-full choice?"

I let it go.

"I'm thinking about something Zeus said. Back at Icarus. Back at training." Ken changed the subject.

"What?" Amira asked.

"That we all decide on the rules of war, on each side." He looked meaningfully at the flashes on Saturn. "How do you think the Conglomeration will take this? How does that figure into their plans when deciding the next stage of the war against us?"

"The shit's always been this deep between them," Amira said. "We're just now getting caught in the middle."

There was a stain spreading across the face of Saturn: the Accordance weapon spreading. Leaping from organic molecule to molecule. Growing. Eating anything in its way and chewing through the howling winds. Down there, anything living was being consumed and burned, the energy from its death fueling the leap to the next target.

I faced away from Saturn with a shiver and looked into the clean darkness of space. Toward the tiny blue glint I had come from. Things might be getting worse. But we were going home.

Home to Earth.

30

Negotiations began in earnest a day before the Pcholem swung us past the moon and into Earth orbit. They continued even as we fell through the upper atmosphere and down into the blue and the white fluffy clouds of Earth. So vibrant. So rich compared to the orange-saturated hues we'd been living in for so long.

So far removed from the landscapes we'd been fighting in.

And then, underneath us, human steel cities glinting in the sun. Beautiful even when scarred by the gouged-out chunks of matte-black Accordance areas, punctured by their organic thorns of skyscrapers built far higher than human reach, from where they could look down upon us. Over the ruins of Washington DC, flashing past Baltimore, and then approaching New York until we flared out over Pelham Bay Park.

Outside, as the fields withdrew from us all and curled back up into Happily Slingshot's belly, the rush of air smelled of sweet spring. People dropped to their knees and kissed the grass. Someone found a tree to hug. Disbelieving laughter was everywhere.

“ARE YOU SURE OF YOUR CHOICE?” Happily Slingshot asked, one final time.

“Yes,” I told the Pcholem.

“IT WAS A PLEASURE TO KNOW YOUR UNIQUE SELF.” The living starship left the ground and ghosted over the park’s trees and then curved up into the air as it pulled in tighter and tighter on itself, until the massive behemoth that had taken tens of thousands of us from Titan all the way to Earth was little bigger than a pair of jumpships.

It pierced a cloud and disappeared, leaving the massive crowd of humanity on the grass.

As per my conditions, I’d shucked my armor, leaving it thirty paces away. Amira and Ken as well. CPF squads surrounded us, rifles out, keeping the blue-suited crowd back and away. “Disperse!”

And bit by bit, the crowds did just that.

A hopper landed at the edge of the park after coming in low over the trees. Jumpships, belly cannon dropped and swiveling in to target us, came next. The crowds surged to run. Off into the trees, out of the park, down the walkways. Nothing good came of a fast, armed Accordance swoop like that.

I kept my arms in the air as the hopper hit the grass, and Colonel Anais stepped out.

I couldn’t help myself. I flinched. Of course.

He glanced at Ken with a flicker of . . . something. Annoyance. Anger. Laying a note down to come back to something, maybe, but other pressing matters needed to be taken care of. The same for Amira, a wry twitch of his lips.

And then Anais stared at me, eye to eye.

“You managed to get them all home, Hart. Congratulations on the biggest PR coup of the war. A hundred thousand men and women, scooped up from the surface of Titan before certain death. All of whom will be able to help us continue the war effort. So, well done."

I didn't answer. To convince the Accordance not to sweep them all up into camps, to come here to this park, for my platoon to not be disciplined, we had to hand ourselves over.

No hiding on the Pcholem. No running.

"You have me; now what?" I asked. "A show trial? And then?"

Anais swept a hand toward the hopper. I stepped in with Amira and Ken. Anais slid the door shut and tapped the bulkhead behind the pilot.

We took off, heading farther into the city, toward Manhattan's core.

"No trial, Hart. You are the destroyer of abominations. The saver of individual lives. The Pcholem love you. Earth loves you. You have a hundred thousand people who owe you their lives. The CPF troops idolize you. Everyone is watching. Closely. No, we bust you down, it's bad PR."

"So, no jail?" I was having trouble wrapping my head around this after spending three days coming to terms with some horrible fate.

"No martyrdom," Anais said. "Something worse. We're going to promote you."

All three of us stared. "Promote?"

"Captain Devlin Hart, Colonial Protection Forces." Anais leaned forward. "Captain. It sounds nice, doesn't it? But it's just a show. We're promoting you so that you're out of trouble's way. Where you can't command any troops to cause any trouble. We're promoting you up so you're going to sit right outside my office where I always have an eye out on you. Me and you, we're going to be like a married couple, Captain. We're going to be joined at the hip, and we're going to use you to raise so many more recruits for the CPF. They're going to line up like screaming tweens for a concert to see you, and you're going to help us send them back out there. Where you can't go anymore."

"And Amira and Ken?"

Anais nodded. "They're going to train the recruits you bring us. After this little flight, the three of you will never be a team again. They will not get promotions. They're lucky to avoid an execution squad."

I glanced at Ken, but his face showed nothing but contempt for Anais.

Anais looked over my armor undersuit and then opened a small can of black grease. He dabbed his thumb in and smeared it randomly across the shoulders and chest. I jerked back when he smudged my chin and cheek. "Verisimilitude," he said.

"What's going on?"

"They all know you've landed. They saw the Pcholem. They know their families came back safe. It's a parade, Captain. They're all here to see their hero. All those potential recruits and citizens grateful to the Accordance." Anais returned the small can of grease to his pocket. "The Conglomeration has abandoned Saturn and its moons. An armada now assembles. It will come for Jupiter. It will come for Mars. It will come for Earth. We live in desperate times, and we need to fight back. Because if we don't, the Accordance will get aboard those Pcholem and leave."

Anais opened the doors. The crowd on the streets around us roared at the glimpse of us.

I turned back to Amira and Ken. "Thank you. For everything."

"Anytime. Anywhere," Amira said, her silver eyes glinting in the dark of the cabin.

"You are my brother," Ken said, reaching out a hand.

Anais pulled me out of the hopper with him before I could say anything more. The hopper screamed and kicked up the air as it lifted off.

I faced the wild crowds, bewildered.

"Now, captain, wave like our lives depend on it," Anais hissed. "Wave like our world depends on it!"

"I don't feel like I deserve any of this," I said.

"You don't," Anais said into my ear. "But wave anyway. Wave for your platoon. Wave for your family. Just wave, dammit."

I raised a hand as confetti showered down on me, the roar of thousands washing past me.

And I waved.

NEW YORK TIMES BESTSELLING AUTHOR
CHUCK
WENDIG
BLACKBIRDS
MIRIAM BLACK KNOWS HOW YOU'RE GOING TO DIE.
"FAST, FEROCIOUS, SHARP AS A SWITCHBLADE, AND F—ING FANTASTIC."
—LAUREN BEUKES AUTHOR OF BROKEN MONSTERS AND THE SHINING GIRLS

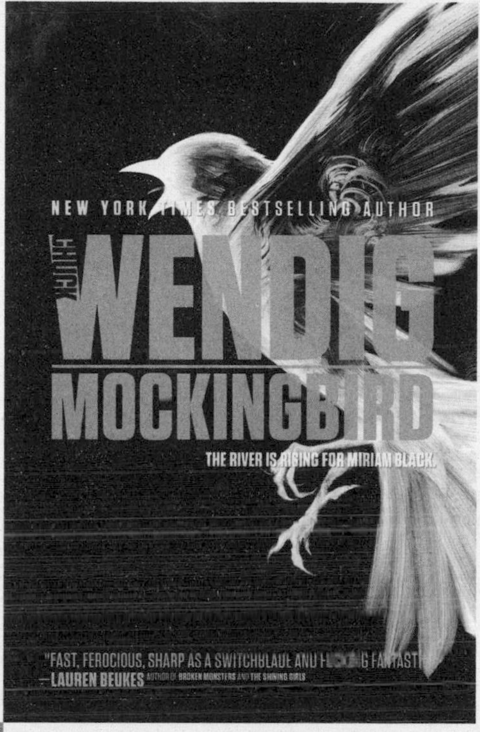
NEW YORK TIMES BESTSELLING AUTHOR
CHUCK
WENDIG
MOCKINGBIRD
THE RIVER IS RISING FOR MIRIAM BLACK.
"FAST, FEROCIOUS, SHARP AS A SWITCHBLADE, AND F—ING FANTASTIC."
—LAUREN BEUKES AUTHOR OF BROKEN MONSTERS AND THE SHINING GIRLS

NEW YORK TIMES BESTSELLING AUTHOR
CHUCK
WENDIG
THE CORMORANT
MIRIAM BLACK HAS TO SOLVE A MURDER BEFORE IT HAPPENS.
"FAST, FEROCIOUS, SHARP AS A SWITCHBLADE, AND F—ING FANTASTIC."
—LAUREN BEUKES AUTHOR OF BROKEN MONSTERS AND THE SHINING GIRLS